I0522345

Medicine Men:

Weeping Eye Dances

by

Donna Amburgey

Book Two, The Red Rock Road Trip

Series

This is a work of fiction. Names, characters, places, and incidents are the products of the author's imagination or are used fictitiously. Any resemblance to actual events, locales, or person, living or dead, is entirely coincidental. Any errors are solely the author's.

Copyright 2014 by Donna Amburgey.

All rights are reserved to the author.

This book was published in the United States by Juke Box Books LLC., St. Charles Illinois

A limited edition of this work will appear in hard copy format. The current publication is in electronic format and soft cover.

ISBN 978-0-9840728-1-1 (soft cover)

Published by Juke Box Books
www.jukeboxbooks.com

Acknowledgements

This book of fiction is the result of my interest in anthropological studies of the cultures of indigenous people of the southwestern United States and other regions. I am indebted to the practicing anthropologists in the early part of the twentieth century who made records of the myths and ceremonies, some of which became a part of this book.

A version of a Cherokee myth explaining the origin of disease and medicine is from "Myths of the Cherokee" by James Mooney, Dover Publications Edition, 1995. A version of a Cherokee children's song featuring Little Bear is derived from the same source.

Excerpts from the Blessing Way, perhaps the best known Navajo ceremonial prayer, derive from research published by Wyman and Kluckhold's in the American Anthropologist Association Publication, 1938.

The description of a Navajo healer's ceremonial acts is based on descriptions from the "Patterns and Ceremonials of the Indians of the Southwest" by Collier and Moskowitz, Dover Publications, 1995 as modified by the author's fictionalization.

I recognize that the healing practices of native healers, sometimes called singers, or medicine men, as described in this book, are largely a cultural or religious feature of the distant past. My intention in incorporating ceremonial information as if it is still a common practice is merely to honor the tradition as a part of the story and as a contrast to the more current practices in medicine.

Dedication

To my most loyal fan and loving husband, Glynn, whose encouragement and proof reading led to a much better book.

Prologue

The casket was gun metal gray and sleek as a missile. Espiritud Soledad-Hotone stood near the head of it beside a lavish spray of red gladioli and white spider mums. The card read "KINGMAN BRICK COMPANY". Smaller tables held more bouquets in tribute to the deceased, but none of them was as large as the one sent by Kingman.

Espiritud--"Sprite" to her legal clients and friends-- recognized almost all of the mourners. Many were Navajo, come to pay respects to the man who had built a clinic near the Reservation. He saved lives their own medicine men could not.

Sprite looked at the line and nodded to Nick Costa, her friend and owner of the Chicken Coop. The restaurant, scarcely more than a diner, would draw many of the mourners into its steamy dining room as the families made their way out of Hidden City after the funeral.

If the deceased had been Navajo there might have been a gathering at a relative's home, with hot clay dishes full of corn and peppers, beans and rice and squash, covered in bright kitchen towels.

But the doctor was not Navajo, and his mourners would not gather in his home but would still feel the need to gather somewhere, even in a restaurant. Nick would not stay for the full service, but would pay his respects in the visitation and then hurry back to the Coop to precook large batches of chicken that could be quickly finished off in the fryer when the rush began.

Sprite glanced again at the casket. She thought about the man who lay there, heavily made up with skin filler to disguise the violence that had ruptured his face just days before. The doctor had been shot at close range with a handgun. The cosmetician did the best she could. Still those who passed by the casket did sly double takes at the face and wondered why it was not quite *him.*

Sprite eyed Deputy Dan Weatherford and knew that his thoughts were elsewhere. Gently she shook his arm and asked him to walk with her to the lounge area. She didn't need to stand so near to the casket. It was the spot traditionally reserved for the widow and other family.

But there was no family. It was as if Dr. Lieber had come out of nowhere: no indication at this lab, in his car, or in his small apartment that he had any family at all. The Navajo police had never seen such a situation. No family? How could a person survive?

As Sprite and Dan sat quietly on the far side of the funeral parlor, Tomas, Sprite's husband, entered the room from a side entrance. He glanced at the corpse, then quickly glanced away. He was not there to engage in false grieving for the dead doctor. He was there to support Spirit, as only he called her.

Tomas was glad that there was no family of the deceased to talk with. He would not have known what to say. Maybe he would have said the wrong thing, like *the last time I saw the doctor, he looked a whole lot worse than he does today.*

Chapter 1

Marcus Steamer gazed at the distant mountain view outside his single office window to calm his racing thoughts. He hefted himself from his chair and felt the low back pain that was getting to be a bigger problem every year. He couldn't make any sense of the recent shooting. He considered himself more experienced than the average detective on the Navajo police force, but he was getting nowhere. Dr. Lieber, from all impressions, should not have had enemies. Surely no one hated him enough to shoot point blank in the face. That was either a statement or an accident. But which?

Marcus ruled out accident. Accidents get reported. People who cause accidents are typically sick to their stomach. They cry, they blame themselves, they run away, but they also turn themselves in within a day or so. No one had come forth to report any accidental shooting of Dr. Terry Lieber.

At least the crime scene was secure. He and Alesha Morgan had gone over the fibers, carefully combing putrid matter into evidence bags. A third technician photographed, measured, and marked the blood spatter for additional analysis. Marcus took the doctor's computer to a secured space. They moved the desk and file cabinet to a locked storage unit.

Marcus pinpointed the basics of what went on in Dr. Lieber's front office the day he was killed. The shooter almost certainly acted alone. Nothing appeared to be disturbed, so robbery was out.

It was easy to locate the two bullets buried in the wall. A third bullet stuck in a skull fragment. The medical examiner would turn it over after he finished his job. The detective found no murder weapon at the scene, but he felt strongly that the gun would surface when the murderer was found.

When the gun was found, it would have a story to tell. From past experience Marcus already knew it was a handgun. The guilty gun would leave a trail of information that Marcus would find. The way the hammer struck the base of any bullet inside would flatten the base, and deform the nose of the bullet in a characteristic way. As the bullet traveled the length of the gun barrel it would continue to warp and to pick up markings, striations, in a spiral pattern, either left or right. A bullet stayed connected to the gun that fired it like a fingerprint. It was not much of a stretch to say that a bullet had someone's name on it, but it was not the victim's name--it was the gun's.

Marcus wrote in his notebook:

Find the gun, find the killer.

The telephone rang, startling Marcus. He picked up the receiver and said, "Steamer."

Dan Weatherford, deputy sheriff in Hidden City, came on the line. Dan's tone was businesslike. He and Marcus knew each other fairly well from working together on a few other shootings that had occurred in Marcus' jurisdiction.

Dan spoke respectfully to Marcus. "I know you're busy and I don't mean to butt in. I just wanted you to know that if you need my help or just someone to talk to about the Lieber killing, I'd be happy to listen."

Marcus was relieved at the offer. He would never have asked for more than the use of the county's lab, but the fact was it could get lonely working a murder. He expected a long journey before this one was solved. His assistant Alesha was as good as they get, but talking to her was not like talking with Dan. She didn't have a long-standing presence in the region, like he and Dan had. She didn't know the people.

"That's a great idea. I would appreciate your take on the crime scene. But I hear that you have your hands full with the Sheriff right now. I don't want to impose."

"He's a handful all right," Dan agreed. "When he was well

he didn't mind leaving most of the details to Tiny Lucas and me. But after all that happened with Tiny I feel like he is looking over my shoulder and second-guessing me. Maybe he just feels like he is losing control."

"He is losing control, Dan, and you know it."

"I shouldn't have said that. Hank is the Sheriff, and when he gets well he will be right back in the driver's seat."

Marcus thought of what he knew of Hank's condition. There was no way he could come back as strong as before. A man held together with gortex arteries might have more time, but not more strength, at his age.

"Dan, when would you be able to take a look at the ballistics report and the scene? I could use your skill with figuring out what kind of gun we should be looking for. I'm having a guy come in to analyze the spatter pattern before we allow any clean up. Maybe you would like to take a look. In this heat, the sooner the better."

"Thanks, Marcus, glad to help. I'll check in with Hank and get the go-ahead, though. I think he'll be able to spare me tomorrow, if I give him a good reason."

"Give me a call when you're on your way. I'm headed back to the evidence warehouse now, to look through his appointment book and bring in the computers. Alesha will help me with that."

"Great. Nice talking with you Marcus. See you tomorrow. Around ten o'clock?"

"Sure, sounds good."

Dan hung up the phone. A rush of adrenaline washed over him. He had to remind himself he was only assisting. Someone else would still be in the driver's seat. Fortunately, it would be Marcus.

Chapter 2

Spirit Soledad-Hotone ran both hands over the heft of her belly as she sat in the only comfortable chair in the house trailer she lived in before Tomas had returned to her life. As a single person who spent more time in her law office than at home, it was spacious enough. But now she and Tomas were cramped.

She was so tired these days--and still had weeks to go before the baby was far enough along to be born. She knew her pregnancy was a text book case; within her womb she carried not only her child but also a tumor. Her obstetrician detected it in her third month and it was keeping pace in growth with the baby.

At her last visit with the doctor he suggested a very early delivery of the baby so that they might tackle the tumor attached to the wall of her uterus. Spirit refused. She would not risk this child, no matter what. Her own life was dear, but if there was to be a choice, let the child live.

Easy enough to say that. But how do I really feel?

"I'm scared to death," Spirit confided to Tomas during one of their late night talks. "But I haven't changed my mind." Tomas looked away and blinked back tears. As a cancer researcher and former surgeon himself, he knew the gravity of his wife's condition. He respected her decision to put the baby's survival first while not yet quite believing that she could actually die from her condition. He looked at her levelly. "Let's talk about something happy," he said. "Happy is good medicine."

Spirit smiled wearily. "Sure, what have you got?"

"How about a dream house by Christmas?"

"That's only weeks away!"

"What if I told you that I've found a place, maybe? Just

what you want: modern, big window looking over a ravine with a spring stream, and everything else. It isn't finished yet but it's started. All of the big stuff is in, and the foundation is poured. The guy who started building it went bankrupt. The mortgage bank wants a quick sale for whatever they can get. I know a carpenter who could finish it. It's up near Desert View by the Canyon.

Spirit looked at her husband in amazement. He would do anything she desired, she thought. He loved her that much.

Her legal mind kicked in, and she sought details. How could a foreclosure sale be done so quickly? There were all those bank procedures.

"But honestly, Spirit, we could see it this evening. Can you drop what you are doing and take a drive?"

Spirit was weak but excited by the news. It had been a while since she had done anything for herself. A new house, everything she dreamed. A baby. A loving husband. A professional life helping those who needed her most. She truly had it all.

"Sure," she said. "Let's go get it."

They approached Desert View in a good mood. The route they has taken led directly through the desert, north by northwest. Spirit noted that no animals had appeared along the way to give them a sign--bad or good. The traffic on the desert road was scant. Spirit asked Tomas to open the car windows and sun roof to feel the cool breeze. The desert air smelled of sage brush.

"What're you thinking about, Spirit?"

"The desert. How I love it. All the mystery locked up in these rocks."

"Could you stand to make this drive often, if you keep the law practice in Hidden City?"

"Oh, it's not so bad. Like I said, I love driving through the desert."

"You will have a little kid to tote around, sometimes."

Spirit was unfazed. "And?" She had watched women tote babies everywhere. She could probably arrange her schedule to a lighter load after the baby was born. Maybe take life a little slower. The thought rested easily on her mind.

She smiled as they pulled onto the construction site. There was no one around and only the rustling of a small animal broke the stillness. Tomas pulled out a 100' measuring tape and began measuring and muttering.

Tomas frowned when he noted the location of the septic field. Where would he put the bigger garage? Even if the septic was of the kind that only needed 10 square feet, it still posed a problem. It might have to be moved.

"I need something to write down some measurements," said Tomas, impatiently.

Spirit handed a pen over. He hadn't asked nicely. Spirit knew he was in his management mode. She tried not to let it rankle. No, she would let it wash over and through her. No hard feelings.

Tomas squinted over his thumb at the far corner of the cleared part of the lot. He estimated the level ground. Another outbuilding or garage would be nice, next year. The space had to be figured now.

He would have to make a list of which cars and motorcycles to bring out from Atlanta. Back there were the treasures from his former life. Most of his luxuries he could let go of for Spirit's world, but he loved his cars. Two more would come soon.

Spirit wandered to the ravine, looking at the space the imagined family room would occupy directly over a fall of water down the rock face. She wanted to be able to watch it flow from a rocking chair. Suddenly she was tired, as if her very bones were calling out to rest there, over the water.

Gazing at the rock walls, she saw there was something scratched into the granite under a tree root. She couldn't make it out, but it was something. Probably graffiti left by a roving group of teenagers. They had the urge and agility to climb even sheer rock to mark their territory, and to impress the girls.

"Spirit? Where'd you go?" Tomas bellowed.

Spirit came back into his view. She loved the property. If Tomas would buy it, they would build her dream house. She could see it in her mind's eye, rising and shining above the tumbling stones of the steep ravine. But she was already worried about keeping the baby, and other future children away from the twenty foot drop off the ravine edge.

Tomas distracted her with his big smile. Apparently he too was satisfied with the rough outlines of the place. He knew how to cut through the purchase process. Money could make magic happen and he needed some magic to close quickly. He would have to offer full price.

"Tomas?" said Spirit softly, "I think this is it. It's everything I dreamed of, right down to the birch trees across the ravine."

Tomas smiled, and again fought back tears. It was perfect. He hadn't been so sure of anything in years.

* * *

It was dark by the time Tomas and Spirit headed back to Hidden City. Spirit was so tired she wanted nothing but sleep. Tomas got out and pulled a small pillow and light blanket from the trunk of the car and tucked her into the front passenger seat.

She was humming her old song, but now with a slower but happier sound. He found himself thinking of the words, in English rather than in the Choctaw that was Spirit's mother's first tongue:

My name is Espiritud/I'm sad and alone/We walk together/and then we run...

Tomas was starting to get it. They would run together, wouldn't they? Spirit's illness could be beaten--he had to believe that. Spirit claimed to know the stakes, but he was pessimistic. He couldn't tell her about his worst fears. Not now. He could only build the house as fast as possible. He needed to reach the carpenter right away. Construction would begin again in ten days, if he had his way.

From his side window, Tomas thought he saw, at the side of the desert highway, a giant deer. It's full rack looked like it had about a five foot spread. Tomas squinted again into clumps of scrubby yew as he passed the spot where he thought he saw the silhouette. Nothing. He smiled, sorry that his wife had missed the vision. Deer were good luck. He sped down the highway.

Spirit slept peacefully, her lips slightly parted. Where she breathed on the window, a light fog grew. Tomas looked on her with love, and admired her bulk under her (his) white T-shirt. Spirit didn't know if she carried a boy or a girl--she said that she didn't want to know, and preferred to be surprised. But Tomas knew. The baby was a girl. And he couldn't be more pleased.

Chapter 3

Waipiti County Assistant Clerk Bonnie Hammer couldn't keep her mind on her work. Her father, Jim Hammer, was clearly not well. He had been going to the doctor off and on. He had lost weight, and he didn't have much spare flesh to begin with. His color was off. He breathed like a man in pain. But he wouldn't tell Bonnie or her mother, Clara, anything besides, "I'll be okay. Don't worry about me. I've been going to the doctor."

And that was it. Clara didn't push, and she held more sway than Bonnie when it came to getting Jim to do whatever it was that she wanted him to do. Bonnie would talk with her mother when Jim was not there.

Bonnie's part-time job in the Clerk's Office was recording marriages, births and deaths. She also ran public notices in the *Pueblo Weekly* paper required by law: foreclosures, name changes, tax sales, estate notices, adoptions, and the like.

The other half time position was in the sheriff's office. She found that job far more interesting than the clerk position. She still handled paperwork that had to be filed at the County by the Sheriff, but it was far juicier: divorce summons, warrants for arrest on failure to appear in court, orders of protection for domestic violence offenses. A lot of times, she knew the people involved, and it always gave her an inner jolt when she read bad things about them. Around the Reservation, everyone knew everyone's business anyway. Gossip grew like weeds despite the general admonition not to talk hard against another person.

But Bonnie believed that people felt better when they shared their sadness and their joy. The concept was the basis for support groups of all kinds from help for nursing mothers, to

Alcoholics Anonymous. The process of coming together on a regular basis and talking about intimate life problems was a tried and true technique for bolstering the spirit.

Her people knew from ancient times the power of gathering, of the supplication of a group for assistance from the Holy People. They knew that sitting around an open fire, telling old stories, and passing tobacco around a healing circle, made miracles happen. Chanting, praying, dancing, as a group, was the standard way of invoking the harmony of nature.

Personal healing, however, required something and *someone* special. For serious illness her people had always looked to the medicine men and hand tremblers. Bonnie remembered trying to explain to Dan Weatherford how it worked in the old days, and how it still worked for many people she knew.

In the past few years it seemed more people were dying than ever before. Many were older, but not *old,* men like her father. Cancer seemed to be the most common cause, lately. She kept an informal watch on the "cause of death" section of the death certificates received from the coroner's office.

Bonnie thought again of her father, and dread filled her mind. She needed to talk with someone--anyone--she was wasting time here at her desk, fidgeting and worrying. She looked at the clock and saw that it was time to get back to work.

* * *

The Sheriff summoned Dan Weatherford via the telephone intercom to step into his office. When Dan arrived Hank gave him a yellow envelope. "Take a look at this," said Hank. "Tell me what you make of it."

Dan studied the confidential inquiry from Kingman Brick Company. It had gone first to the Coroner's Office. The Coroner's Office had apparently made a copy for the eyes of the Sheriff only. It was a request for the names and addresses of any person who had died in the past year of liver cancer, or leukemia. The letter asked the Coroner to keep the inquiry in the strictest confidence.

Dan ventured, "Maybe an insurance claim against the company?"

"Something like that, I guess."

Dan was thinking of something. Liver cancer. Leukemia. "Seems like there have been quite a few cancer deaths in this area in the past few years. For a while I'd hear about somebody dying just about every time I went to the coffee shop. Of course around here that's about all the old guys talk about, anyway. Who is sick, who is dying or dead."

"Yep. I know what you mean. It's depressing is what it is. Sometimes I don't even want to talk to anyone over the age of forty- five."

"We have enough going on with our jobs," said Dan. "Do we really have to get mixed up in something like this?"

"Only if a crime has been committed, as far as I know."

Dan studied the letter from Kingman Brick Company again. He knew the company; it had employed a lot of young men in the sixties when there was high interest in using natural materials in construction all across the country. Business boomed for Kingman Brick Company.

One of Dan's uncles worked at Kingman for a short time, but he had asthma and couldn't handle the dust that swirled off the massive cone shaped heaps of clay that were trucked in daily. Dan clamped the yellow envelope between his elbow and his body to free both hands as he poured himself a cup of coffee from the office pot.

"I'll get on the Kingman letter this afternoon Hank. I'll let you know when I'm done."

"Okay, thanks. I don't know if you know, but the owner of Kingman Brick Company is an old buddy of mine. He helped me get started in politics, even made a couple of good sized campaign contributions when the company was going gangbusters. He's a good guy."

"What's his name again? Sorry, I didn't look that closely at the letter."

"Cal Kingman."

"Okay, I'm on it. Bonnie will be here this afternoon and we'll start going through the records. She can help us out with doing some computer searching.

"Good. I have to get going now. There is a barbecue lunch at the Rotary that I don't want to miss."

"Boy that sounds good. I guess I'll go out to the Coop. The rooster plate sounds good to me. See you later."

* * *

Dan returned as Bonnie was just walking in the door. She glanced at Dan and thought how much she liked seeing him. He was married and she wasn't, so they kept a professional distance.

Dan liked Bonnie too. She was pretty and hardworking. She watched out for her son Clay, taking the child in for vaccinations and making sure there was food in the house. She lived with her mother, Clara and her father, Jim.

Dan knew that Bonnie's family had gone through hard times before Jim had stopped drinking. At the bottom of those times, Jim's doctor told him that if he didn't stop drinking he was going to die. And soon. His liver was starting to fail and his blood pressure soar. Jim stopped drinking and started attending AA and became chapter leader.

He and Clara started laughing together again, and Jim found work that he could do at the National Park. He was hired as a guard at one of the larger Anasazi ruins. He made sure that no visitor picked up any pottery shards that were supposed to rest in place at the ancient home sites. He kept people from walking on the tops of the thick walls of the pueblo ruins. Jim constantly warned people trying to pry the lid off the desert blowhole that was located in the courtyard of the settlement, preventing them from dropping coins down the hole. It was a pretty good job. Clara at the time was building her own life, as a healer and a midwife.

But Jim started to lose weight for no reason around the time he had started working as a guard. The Park Service let him wear a gun belt and service revolver after his training, more for the possibility of having to shoot a big rattler than out of concern that the tourists would require that level of persuasion. Jim said if it was all the same to them he would like to have his own weapon that he had carried for nearly thirty years. It was a Smith & Wesson .357 Magnum, and it fit his hand like a firm handshake.

He had not been on the job long before he noticed that he had to move the buckle in to the next hole for the belt to fit right. Jim was pleased at first, he had started to get a middle-aged spread in his hips, and he had always prided himself on his long, lean silhouette. His belly was puffy—but hell all the men his age had some gut. For as much alcohol as he had drunk, he had been largely spared the taut stomach bulge that usually advertised one's drinking habits.

But soon he had to take the gun belt in another notch. He noticed that he was as tired in the morning as he was after a day's work. Something wasn't right. Unknown to his wife and daughter--they were such worriers--he saw Dr. Lieber one evening after he had finished his guard duty.

Dr. Lieber scared him with his comments. He would have to run some tests, blood tests and urine tests and stool tests. After those came in they would probably need to do scans of his internal organs. The doctor pushed his fingers deep into Jim's sides, and pushed hard on his groin. He frowned while Jim winced in pain.

* * *

Bonnie listened as Dan Weatherford explained a project that involved going back into death records for the County and pulling out those that listed cancer as the cause of death. Dan, in his conscientious way, asked Bonnie to pull out all records of deaths related to cancer for the county for the past five years.

"That'll be easier to do on my computer at the Clerk's office," she said.

As she said it, she thought of all the names she already knew, because they were people that she or her family had known. Images of men her father's age and older flashed through her memory: Lally Garver, Bob Springer, Henry Tribble, and

Sam--what was his last name--she couldn't remember. So maybe it had not been her imagination that there seemed to be an outbreak of cancer deaths.

Please God don't let my dad be one of them.

Chapter 4

Sheriff Andrews picked up the telephone, called information, and wrote down a number for Kingman Brick Company. He hadn't talked to Cal Kingman in many years. Besides being curious about the letter he received he was interested in catching up on his old friend and campaign contributor.

A female voice answered the phone after three rings. Hank asked for Cal Kingman and she hesitated.

"Who's calling?"

"Sheriff Hank Andrews."

"May I tell him why you're calling?"

"No, I can tell him myself. Is he there or not?"

"I'll check."

A moment later Cal picked up. "Hank Andrews? Waipiti County's finest?"

"Yep, that's me. How the hell are you, Cal?"

"I've been better, Hank."

"I just got the letter you wrote to the coroner here. Looking for information about cancer deaths in the county."

"I thought we sent that to the coroner, not the sheriff."

"He knows I like to know about everything that goes on here. He sent it to me. What's this all about? I thought you were busy getting rich making bricks."

"Well we're not as busy as we used to be, but we're surviving."

"And this stuff about cancer?"

"The State Environmental Board is asking for that."

"Why?"

"A lawyer wrote me a letter a few months ago. Claims that a doctor up in your area--maybe near the Reservation--filed a report about a suspicious number of deaths from some kind of cancer. The thing these guys had in common was they worked at our plant twenty or thirty years ago. Trying to show a link between the thorium dust that came in here with truckloads of sand back in the sixties, and the workers' getting cancer years later. I've been doing nothing besides trying to satisfy the regulators of the mine tailings and now this big investigation about cancer."

Hank felt sorry for his friend. "That's rough," he said. What's the doctor's name?" Is he from Hidden City?"

"No, I don't think so--let me see --."

Hank heard papers rustling.

"Here it is…Dr. Terry Lieber."

"Oh sure, I've heard of him. Even met him once at a Rotary breakfast. Seemed like an okay guy. I know a lot of the families on the Reservation doctor with him."

Cal breathed out a sigh. "I haven't had a decent night's sleep in weeks because of this. What they are saying is that back before we had to treat the tailings from the soil--going back to the fifties and sixties--hell I don't even know, the miners and workers breathed in the dust. On a really windy day it looked like a dust storm out by the sand yards. Now some of my workers are getting leukemia and other cancers, I could understand lung cancer--and I guess there is that too--but leukemia and liver cancer. You know, most of the guys are heavy smokers too. It was different in those days. Nobody worried about these things."

Hank grunted agreement. "It's gone too far in my opinion. How's the little guy supposed to compete with the giant mining companies? I saw that report of Mining Standards from the Clean Air Department. Now I'm not saying we shouldn't protect the water--I drink it too. But who could follow all the legal procedures for lining filtration ponds and covering ore heaps; even planning against *earthquakes* for Pete's sake."

"Tell me about it. Sure I know the report. Three hundred pages of requirements. Now I know there is radioactive material in the dirt and clay I've always used--I have regular inspections from the agencies--I wish I had never gotten into this crazy business!"

Hank was sympathetic. Every time he turned around prisoners were getting more rights. If you had to shoot someone best be prepared to explain it to a jury later. He was glad to be getting on, ready for retirement.

"So anyway this Dr. Lieber seems like a real crusader for finding out exactly what happened to my workers back then. How much thorium they were exposed to, mainly. Plus what ran into the water. I'm on the hot seat."

"You used to be a hero, Cal. You gave people good jobs and paid them fairly. Don't beat yourself up."

"I'm going to look into this from here, Cal. I'll follow up on Dr. Lieber and try to get a handle on what's going on. I'll let you know."

"Thanks, Hank."

"Happy to help. You watch yourself now. This bullshit will pass. Don't let it get to you." As he spoke he reached for his Smith and Wesson and holstered it. It was a habit with the Sheriff when he went anywhere, even the Rotary barbecue.

Chapter 5

Dr. Terry Lieber peered into his microscope at the tissue sample taken from his patient's liver. It didn't look good. Jim Hammer had liver cancer; that was for sure. Years of drinking had etched a roadmap onto Jim's face in the form of broken capillaries and saggy, stretched skin--or perhaps that was the result of drinking instead of eating proper food. Now, in his sixties, the body evidenced his multiple bad habits.

Dr. Lieber asked his nurse to call Jim and ask him to come in as soon as he could. There would be more tests: more blood work, CT scans, probably additional biopsies. Dr. Lieber studied Jim's file again. Would he be candidate for Dr. Lieber's research? And had he ever worked for Kingman Brick Company?

Dr. Lieber made some notes in the computer file. Then he went to his locked filing cabinets and unlocked it. The top drawer contained the files of seven men and two women who had worked at Kingman Brick Company. All of them were dead now. All had formed the study population for his work on a cure for cancer. He had hand-picked the group as he treated his largely Navajo patient population.

Dr. Lieber's work was secret. He had told no one of his attempts to find a cure for cancer. When he eventually found the cure, the world would forgive him for what he did to those seven people.

He was getting close, he sensed it. And for now, he was able to throw off any possible suspicion by taking the offensive. He was taking the lead on investigating a brick manufacturing plant. As it turned out, the brick material contained thorium. It was assumed to emit radiation at such a low level that it was not deemed a health hazard at the time. Now, of course, the scientific community knew better. And the residents, those who had worked in the brick factory years ago--they knew better too.

By now the information has leaked out to the people on the Reservation that the dust they breathed back then had poisoned them, and was in their blood still in the form of leukemia. And probably lung and liver cancer too. Dr. Lieber, through his careful questioning of his patients - *Did you ever work for Kingman Brick Company, or any other brick making plant?* - only planted the suggestion in his patients' that there was a connection—and gossip and fear carried the patient to the next level. By the time of the second visit to Dr. Lieber, they were sure that they had breathed in the dust and drank the water and shoveled the tailings and operated the bulldozer and loaded the bricks day after day and even year after year.

Dr. Lieber got to be the hero. He was actively taking on Kingman Brick Company down at the statehouse and in the EPA and anywhere that he could. He was interviewed by progressively bigger media outlets, then the television crews began to call on him. The plan worked even better than he had ever imagined.

Chapter 6

The tumor growing silently and steadily alongside the child in Spirit's womb might as well have ticked like a time bomb, in Tomas' mind. He tried to keep Spirit busy and entertained with the details of the home construction, while his thoughts were consumed with the delayed treatment of his wife's precarious condition. He loved her for her dedication to the unborn child, but he often awakened in the middle of the night with a jolt and then a racing heart and his dark thoughts about her prognosis.

Sometimes he imagined that his grandfather was with him during his night terror. Tomas often got up out of bed and went outside, and looked at the sparkling heavens, and talked to his grandfather's spirit.

"What should I do, Jawotnehe," he begged.

"Cure her."

"I don't think that I can,"

"Then you will certainly fail."

"I will have to leave her alone if I try to find a cure. What if something should go wrong while I'm gone?" asked Tomas.

One night Tomas was pacing in the gravel drive outside the trailer under a new moon. His head was full of ideas. He could take Spirit with him—but she would probably refuse to be budged from her office and clients. Then he had an idea. He could find someone to watch out for Spirit while he traveled back to Atlanta to consult with other cancer surgeons. He thought over some possible friends: Nick Costa from the restaurant?

Too busy, he concluded.

Then it came to him: Deputy Dan Weatherford. He knew

that Dan Weatherford had a soft spot for Spirit; he could sense it whenever they were all together. He could see it in Dan's eyes when Spirit walked up to join them over coffee at the Coop. Such little things that mean so much if one knows how to read them.

All he needed was for Dan to check on Spirit every day and see how she was feeling. If there was a problem, Dan could easily contact Tomas by cell phone. Tomas would of course tell Spirit what he had in mind and she would protest that she didn't need a babysitter --and maybe she didn't--but Tomas was not willing to take the chance. Spirit didn't know of the life-threatening possibilities of her illness, and Tomas felt it was better for her to not know. The stress of knowing would be detrimental to her health; at the very least her immune system might become compromised. Spirit needed all of her reserves right now.

* * *

After making the arrangements, Tomas left for Atlanta. He called up a former colleague and arranged to have lunch with him as soon as he arrived.

On the flight Tomas slept badly, dreaming of a powerful figure, dark and massive about the shoulders and neck. It seemed to change from his grandfather's shape to a large brown bear. It spoke in low, short tones, perhaps in a variant of his native Cherokee, perhaps in animal sounds. The shape pushed at Tomas' chest with strong limbs and prodded him with its thick head, like it wanted Tomas to wake up. When he finally did, his chest felt sore and he felt exhausted, beaten up.

In his half awake, half asleep daze, Tomas thought about the dream. *What was Jawotnehe up to? What was he trying to tell him?* The bear was understandable: it was in his totem, a spirit guide. Tomas' personality was indeed like that of a bear. He liked going into a cave-like solitude. He did his best thinking in a darkened office or workshop, and preferred to spend long periods of time ruminating on a problem, rooting around for a solution. He believed he gained his wisdom in silence—much like a hibernating bear, he tended to curl up under a heavy blanket and think before going into long stretches of sleep. It was difficult to wake him during those deep sleeps, and if he was awakened too soon, he was cross until he was ready to be awake on his own terms.

Tomas thought of the bear's head bashing into him and decided it was simply a connection to his own feeling that he had been banging his head against a wall of frustration in his inability to be a full physician to Spirit. His terror over the possibility of losing her, and his lack of access to the facilities at a first rate hospital that would provide the tools to give her the best of care, had acted in tandem to freeze any action on his part. *Enough, Tomas thought. I've got to take action. I only hope it is not too late.*

* * *

He saw the familiar skyline of Atlanta as the plane approached Hartsfield Airport and banked into the landing pattern. The flight activity was such that they would circle the airport many times before it was their turn to be cleared for landing. Tomas had been away from such ramped up action for so long that it was noticeable, and irritating. He had grown accustomed to the laid back pace of the desert, the silence of the sun and clouds as they passed overhead against a cobalt sky, day after day. When he walked into the terminal he could smell the crowd. People filled the seats and overflowed onto the floor space, backs leaned into the plate glass windows overlooking the airfield; babies cried and old people were parked in wheelchairs like baggage to be loaded onto the jumbo jets going everywhere, all day and all night. It was an assault on Tomas' senses.

He was not feeling well, and the fouled air of the airport wasn't helping any. He realized that he had not eaten anything worthwhile since Spirit made a steak for him the night before. He hurried into a restaurant at the airport. Normally Tomas would not have considered eating at the airport restaurant but he went from hungry to very hungry in what felt like his system downshifting into low gear.

Once inside he found a table for two and asked the drink server to send the waitress quickly. The place was packed and Tomas wanted to get his order in right.

Tomas found no comfort in the metal café chairs that crowded the dining area. He was shifting his weight against the unyielding narrow seat when a dark man sat next to him. The dining room was so small and packed that there was less than a foot between them. Tomas noticed that the man had the facial structure of a native Cherokee like his own ancestors. He dressed casually, but neatly. His thick straight hair was tied back with a leather string. The man took in Tomas' appearance and nodded. Tomas nodded back.

The throng in the restaurant had raised the noise to an uncomfortable level. Conversation was not possible; one had to yell. Tomas was vaguely disappointed; he might have struck a pleasant conversation with the man next to him. Instead, he was left with his thoughts. He remembered his dream on the plane, and was suddenly struck by a story that he remembered hearing from Jawotnehe, or at least he thought he remembered. Perhaps it was his father who had told it: the story of the origins of medicine and disease.

Tomas had not thought of this story in a very long time -- since medical school, most likely--but as the stranger next to him sat quietly, his gaze directed into the clanking crowd, Tomas remembered it all:

There was a time when all of the animals and even the plants, could talk to each other. At first the human beings were few in numbers, but as time went on, there were more and more people. The animals were alarmed because the people were crowding them and killing them for food and for their hides.

Finally the animals were fed up enough to go to council. The bears held the first council. Among themselves they spoke and concluded that man had to be dealt with just as man dealt with them. Other animals held their own councils with similar results...no one could think of a solution. In the end the animals began to curse man, calling down disease after disease to weaken the human beings.

The plants were silent. The human beings didn't kill the plants, preferring the meat of animals. The plants felt sorry for the human beings and for the curses that had been laid upon them. The plants determined to befriend the humans, and to give them their plant gifts, all of which had particular uses in curing disease. But they would not talk with the humans. Rather, they would be willing to give their healing powers when the humans figured out the special powers of each plant. The trees, shrubs and even down to the grasses and mosses promised to defeat each disease that the animals had rained down on humans, but only if the people respected the wisdom of the plants.

And then either his grandfather or his father told him: *When the doctor does not know what medicine to use for a sick man, the spirit of the plant tells him.*

Tomas looked at the crowd around him and smiled. The dream of the bear butting into him was simply his ancestor's spirit reminding him of the old Cherokee myth of disease and plant medicine.

Buoyed with new confidence, Tomas worried less about Spirit's cure. It was out there. All he had to do was to find it.

Ancient wisdom told him he wouldn't find it in the laboratories in Atlanta. There was no need after all to begin research there or in a modern hospital. The cure would be found instead in a forest, or perhaps in the desert right under his nose.

For the first time in a long time, Tomas relaxed. He would enjoy his dinner, and then rest in the apartment that he still had in Atlanta. He would meet his former associate for lunch and catch up on the latest news and gossip. Then he would get busy with his plan to find a way to defeat Spirit's illness that would be safe for her and the child.

The man sitting next to him got up and with another nod of his head and a small tight smile on his lined face, left the restaurant.

* * *

The next day Atlanta was covered in a light fog. The

temperatures were only in the fifties and a slow drizzle began as Tomas began to prepare for the day. From his mullioned windows Tomas saw the broad, tree-lined avenue, the pavement glistening from the rain as vapor rose in patches from the black asphalt. There was little traffic; it was too early for workers to begin their dash to the offices. Tomas' mental list of tasks drew him from bed to kitchen to start a pot of coffee and to boot up his laptop computer. First on the list was to call Spirit and wish her good morning. Second was to call Ed and inquire about the status of the building of the house in Desert View.

Tomas had last seen the house on Sunday. He remembered the weather; it was a sunny, slightly windy day. The morning air in the hills was cold, but as the sun rose higher he was warmed and by noon he had to peel off his outer, long sleeved denim shirt. He and Ed checked the orientation of the house and the placement of the windows in the family room high over the ravine. They were to be built to capture the full rays of the sun as it rose over the distant canyon walls in the wintertime, while set in enough beneath the ledge of the second story to be shaded in the summertime.

Tomas reached Ed through a static filled connection. "Everything's fine here," Ed said. "What's new in Atlanta?"

Tomas was cheerful, excited about something. "I'm having a quick lunch with an old friend from the Medical Center here. I thought I might need to stay a while but I really don't. I'm picking up one of my cars from storage, taking it in for quick oil change and checkup, then I'm hitting the road."

Ed perked up. Tomas had talked to him before about his car collection. He had described the six cars in such loving detail that Ed felt he knew them personally. "What are you bringing out?" Ed asked.

Tomas never hesitated. There was only one choice, his Aston Martin Vanquish. He needed its power and speed to get back to Arizona as fast as possible. He had work to do there that wouldn't wait.

The Vanquish. Slick as a cold liqueur. Fast like mercury.

Just as deadly if not respected. If anything could be his steed on his quest to vanquish Spirit's deadly tumor, it was the Aston Martin. His next call would be to the garage porter to bring it up, and then to Frank Spitzer to arrange lunch. Suddenly he was starved.

* * *

Tomas and Frank decided on the First Page, a newspaper themed second story restaurant with a first rate salad bar. The choice of cold sliced ham, turkey or beef and deviled eggs with salsa were enough to make a meal, but then came the vegetable selections: deep fried okra or mushrooms. Broccoli and cheese casserole, pasta primavera, cold asparagus tips with hollandaise, homemade pickles. Corn on the cob or corn soufflé, and then lettuce salad, plus warm muffins.

Frank quizzed him about his unexpected return to Atlanta. Everyone at the research facility where Frank and Tomas had once worked knew that Tomas had escaped the city and found love in the desert. Those who knew him well knew how happy he was. He was in love, and there was never a contest between real love and a job one had to do for a paycheck. Tomas no longer required a paycheck, and that too made him a free and happy man.

Tomas spoke lightly but efficiently of Spirit's tumor. Frank was a surgeon and not a delicate man, so Tomas was not worried about offending him at lunch by discussing biopsies, tumor stages, blood work, and treatment options. Frank sat and listened and then suddenly snapped his fingers as if something had snapped into place. "You know there is a brilliant cancer researcher in northern Arizona. He is aggressive, too. I hear he is going after the mining companies that exposed workers to thorium and uranium years ago. And he can't be that far from where you are. I think his clinic is near one of the Indian Reservations. What's his name...I've read some papers he wrote when he testified at a congressional hearing...oh hell, I can't think of it."

Tomas mind was working hard. "Oh, yeah, I think I know

who you mean."

He had read something in the Pueblo News recently, but had not realized that the doctor who was the subject of the local article was so well known. But if the doctor was that hot, he probably had a good lab. A cancer researcher simply could not exist without a state of the art lab. He would find him. When the need arose, and if he could save time by using another doctor's lab, that would be a great help. He would pay the man well for the privilege.

Frank said, "I'll call you later on your cell phone with the name. I know where that article is, on my desk."

"Thank you," he said. "Let me get the check." His mind had moved on to the open road, and going home to Spirit.

Frank reached to cover Tomas' hand. "Just a second. There is one more thing. You remember our side business…well I'm started to feel a little heat from our investors. The big ones."

Tomas looked at him levelly. "Not good news."

Frank had just given him one more reason to leave town again, and quickly.

Chapter 7

It was noon at the Coop, and the colder October winds blew more than the usual number of customers into the steamy dining room to eat hot fried chicken, fried corn bread, black beans and slaw. Truckers dallied a little longer with the cute new waitress, begging for another refill of the strong dark coffee. When Gigi was done with the guy she just sent Possum around with the next pot. He had no problem telling the customer that *this is the last one I'm giving you.* Possum had no capacity at all for sweetening reality.

Nick kept Possum around for just such moments. The new waitress was still too farm fresh to stand up to the more obnoxious regulars. She expected to take a certain amount of leering--at eighteen, she already knew she drew mens' looks--and Nick told her that in a restaurant most of the fun for the regulars was flirting with cute waitresses. It was like a tavern in that way for those who couldn't go out at night; they had wives and kids at home.

The wives knew that even if their husbands did go out, they couldn't handle a night of drinking like they could have when they were eighteen, or twenty-one, or twenty-nine. The exceptions were the hard core drinkers, those who graduated early into alcoholism. They could stay out all night, and often did. Eventually, they came home to an empty house or trailer.

Nick had no mercy for the drunks. He worked so hard himself that he couldn't understand anyone who didn't have the same view of what it took to run a business or stick with a job. To work was to live and to live was to work, to Nick. It was that simple. So what if your face became haggard and your back hurt

--you worked. And you kept your complaints to yourself.

The new girl was all cheeks and fine baby blonde hair that sometimes fell across her forehead so that she had to push it away from her face. Nick wanted her to wear a hairnet but she looked at him with those huge blue eyes and just rolled her eyes. He stepped back: should he take such insolent behavior from this little girl? They settled on her wearing a Nets ball cap. He wanted her to wear a waitress uniform but she claimed she was allergic to nylon and nobody had to wear those stupid things anymore. They settled on jeans that didn't show too much of her cute belly button, and a white tee shirt that didn't show too much of her high breasts.

Nick allowed Possum to refill the coffee cups after the second round from Gigi --the name that Grace Rutherland had given herself when she became a waitress. She had found a rhinestone studded pin with the name Gigi spelled out in cubic zirconium and decided it was cool enough to wear on her Nets cap.

Possum adored Gigi. Now that Sprite was married he had moved on to silently being in love with the waitress who was younger than he was, but seemed to know so much about the world. Gigi told him she was always reading magazines about how to improve yourself. Maybe he could do that too she said. She saw a project in Possum, and did her best to teach him. He was a more than willing student.

* * *

Dan Weatherford climbed out of his squad car and ambled in to the Coop. He settled himself in the usual booth, pushing aside Nick's ledger and newspaper. Out of the corner of his eye he watched Gigi. She'd seen him come in and brought him a chipped mug and the coffee pot.

Dan laid the file folder he had brought in with him on the table and smiled at Gigi. "What should I have?" he asked her.

"Well you usually have the Rooster plate, don't you?" she replied.

"I do, but I don't know about that today."

"Okay, so what do you want?"

"A cheeseburger."

"All right. How do you want it cooked?"

"Burn it a little."

She checked off *well done.* Nick would know what to do.

The door pushed open and Dan saw a tall thin man come in. Something was familiar about him--then he saw that he was looking at Jim Hammer, He'd heard from Bonnie at the clerk's office that her dad was sick, but it looked to Dan like Jim was past *sick.*

Jim nodded to Deputy Weatherford. Dan motioned with a flick of his head for Jim to have a seat. He felt like having company.

Jim walked over and lowered himself gingerly into the booth. Dan could feel the man's aches and exhaustion. Dan put out his hand to shake Jim's toneless hand. Jim pushed the brim of his cowboy hat up, then remembered to take it off. He combed his thinning hair back with his fingers.

Dan looked into sunken eyes and fearful eyes. "Jim," he said, "where have you been keeping yourself? I haven't seen you for I don't know how long."

"I'm working now, up at the National Park. I'm a guard."

"Well that's great. How is Clara?"

"She's fine. I'm the one falling apart, I guess."

Sprite Soledad entered the dining room from the back rear hallway door. She didn't have far to walk; her small office was a remodeled back addition to the restaurant. It was a good thing because she was carrying quite a bit of weight on her body from the pregnancy. Dan gave her a two finger salute and she came over to the table.

Dan moved over to make room for Sprite. She couldn't simply slip into a booth the way she used to. Now she more or less lowered herself and plopped in sideways before rotating her hips and legs to fit snugly under the diner table. Next month she would have to pull a chair up to the end of the table like the people who were enormously overweight. Getting up was getting to be a problem for her, too. She leaned over and patted Jim's arm, "How are you?" she asked.

Jim and Dan knew that it was a real question, not just a traditional "Hi how are you" ritual that nobody answered candidly. *Fine* was the expected reply.

She waited for Jim to compose his mouth. She saw the tremble and guessed he had something on his mind.

Gigi brought Dan's food just then and took orders from Jim and Sprite. Dan started to wait but realized his burger would be stone cold by the time their lunches were ready. He excused himself for not waiting, and they said "Oh, no, just go on ahead." Dan bit in to the perfectly cooked burger and hot cheese topping.

Jim was grateful for the interruption. He felt a little shaky. Now he could speak without his voice giving him away. And he knew these people could be trusted.

"I've been better," he said.

Spirit stayed his arm. She knew how it felt to be sick, and how difficult it was to judge when to talk about it, when to keep it to one's self. She had enough practice at this herself with her own medical condition. Her decision had been to tell no one, except of course, Tomas. Dan Weatherford knew that she had problems of some kind but Spirit didn't know that Tomas had confided quite a bit of detail in Dan. Everyone needed to talk to at least one person, it seemed. Jim chose to lay out his problem to Dan and Sprite.

"Things are not great," Jim began. "Maybe you heard something from Bonnie. I know she is worried sick about me. I haven't outright told her or Clara but I guess I'll have to soon. I have cancer in my liver and maybe some other places."

Sprite placed her hand on his arm and held it firmly. "I'm so sorry, Jim."

Dan winced and thought about Bonnie. All she had talked about when they were going through the files for the information that the sheriff had requested on local cancer deaths, was her dad. She told Dan how her dad had lost so much weight, and never had any appetite, and was so dead tired all the time.

Looking at the man before him, Dan could understand Bonnie's fears.

Sprite spoke up. "You are getting treatment though, aren't you Jim?"

"I've been up to see that doctor up by the Reservation several times. I just don't tell Clara or Bonnie. They would just worry themselves sick, and one sick person in the family is enough."

"What doctor is that?" asked Sprite.

"His name is Dr. Lieber. He is supposed to be a real hot-shot cancer doctor. I don't know why he works so far out in the middle of nowhere."

"What does Dr. Lieber have to say, if you don't mind my asking," Dan said.

"He has me on some medicine or supplements or something that's supposed to increase my immunity. Injections. Eventually there will be surgery and chemotherapy and radiation and I don't know what all. I'm going to have to tell Clara and Bonnie soon, I know. I've just been putting it off. The thing is, I've never had any insurance. So who is going to pay for all that treatment? I have talked to Dr. Lieber about that, and he is trying to get me some help from somewhere."

Sprite was genuinely impressed. "What else do you know about the man?"

"Oh he's really great. I heard about him at AA. He was treating Lally when he died, and some of the other Navajos. Dan now remembered seeing Dr. Lieber's name on the death certificates of most, maybe all of the people who had died of cancer in the area. Bonnie had mentioned how odd it was that the same doctor always signed the certificate. It didn't seem that odd to Dan Weatherford, especially if the guy was a specialist. How many other cancer specialists were practicing in that part of the state?

Sprite's mind was working hard on an idea. She knew that she needed specialized care, and soon. Maybe Dr. Lieber could help her, with injections, to keep the tumor growth in check until the baby was born. She didn't want to offend Tomas. He had wanted to treat her himself but she at that point was content to receive no treatment. But it wouldn't hurt to get a second opinion from this other doctor. She decided to see Dr. Lieber before Tomas returned from Atlanta. That gave her about two days.

* * *

Gigi showed up with the lunch orders for Sprite and Jim. Sprite was grateful for a distraction from the talk of illness. Jim seemed relieved to have opened up to someone. He felt that he would be able to tell his wife and daughter what he knew as soon as he got back home. Soon the talk turned to the usual subject: the weather. It had been a hotter than usual summer and fall and that led to the usual lightning strikes and forest fires a little further north, up in the forested hills near the Canyon. Sprite thought of their new home that was growing closer to completion every day. She had been talking with the carpenter, Ed, at least twice a week as he and his crew worked on the progressive stages of construction. At the rate they were going Tomas and Sprite might be able to move in by Christmas. She was so excited and consumed with the hundreds of decisions to be made for the completion of each room. The trailer was piled high with decorating books and paint samples, and furniture catalogs.

Their home would be just beautiful, with everything she had always dreamed of. Inside would be their happy little family. She imagined rocking her baby in a wooden rocking chair, before the stone fireplace, as the snow fell softly and piled up deep in the ravine. Suddenly she couldn't wait for Tomas to come home.

Chapter 8

Bonnie Hammer made two copies of each death certificate she found in which the deceased had died of cancer. In reading the reports she began to note that one doctor in particular, Dr. Terry Lieber, had signed nine of the certificates. The dates on the certificates went back about ten years and in that time fourteen deaths were recorded. She slipped one set of the copies into an unmarked folder and put the folder into her woven bag. The other set she put in an interoffice memo envelope that she would give to Dan Weatherford.

Bonnie resolved to call Dr. Lieber and set up an appointment for her father. Something had to be done. He was wasting away. Her father, a tall man, had always seemed indestructible to her. Just being around him made her feel protected. Now his jeans hung off his hips and his muscle tone was gone from his arms and shoulders.

There was another call to be made as well. Bonnie had saved up for a healing ceremony. She called the preeminent "singer" on the Reservation to begin the negotiations concerning the duration, content and location of the healing ceremony that she had in mind for her father. The options ranged from a three day chant to a nine day chant. As sick as her father was Bonnie was not sure that anything less than a full nine day Night Way chant, one of the Holy Way ceremonials, would do. The ceremony would no doubt include a selection from the Blessing Way, to correct any errors that may have crept in to the chant or the sand paintings.

Bonnie left a message on Hosteen Clah III's answering machine. She described briefly her interest in holding a healing ceremony for her father. She assured the healer of her ability to pay.

Clah arranged to meet with Bonnie at her family's home over the weekend. There he would view the inside of the home, inquire about how many relatives were available to host the healing, and determine the size of the crowd that might gather. A sand painting healing was a public event and so the host family had to be prepared to feed many people. And Clah himself would have to be adequately compensated.

"My father is ill, Hosteen," said Bonnie, "I think he must have cancer or something because he had lost so much weight."

"I and my assistants will sing to attract good," said the healer. "The hand trembler will diagnose, and I will treat your father."

Clah went said, "But for such a serious illness surely the nine day ceremony will be needed. "

"What kind of painting will you do?" Bonnie asked. She was thinking that they would need to use a neighboring hogan to accommodate the size of the required sand painting. Eight feet by eight feet was what she expected.

"If I had to guess right now I suspect it would be the Father Sky, Mother Earth at a minimum," Clah said. "This is why I need to see the hogan."

Hosteen Clah III would decide. He was a master weaver as well as a healer, but that didn't capture the essence of his power. His father and grandfather were esteemed healer/singers which added to his reputation. His textiles sold to museums for shocking amounts of money.

Clah sang at every Blessing Way or Holy Way chant that he performed. His chorus consisted now of fewer and fewer singers as the youth drifted into more Western ways. He needed a substantial backup chorus to sound an effective Talking God's Song or the Companion Calling God's Song. *How could a lone voice expect to imitate God? Or to reach God's ears? No one acting alone could expect success, one needed community for any effective result. The whole: so much greater than any one acting alone.*

Bonnie asked about the Night Way possibilities: could a nine day ceremony to be spread over the coming weeks so as to satisfy the need for repetition? Again, Clah admonished her over trying to set that in advance.

"God alone knows," he said. Then he said something in his native dialect that Bonnie could not understand.

Bonnie agreed to discuss the details in person at their home. A meeting was set.

She didn't begrudge him his fee: the healer himself has to go through an arduous cleansing process: three days of purification-fasting, vomiting, purgatives until his mind and body were clean of any human process. He would gather the raw materials for sand painting-corn, plant ochres, soil and mineral elements, all powdered to raw colorful grains that would be trickled in colorful and intricate ritual patterns.

The ill person would be seated to the east, there to remain for the required time for healing as determined by the singer. There were options of prayer sticks, token tying, offerings to be made, and the all night singing, night after night. A successful healer studied for years for his profession, assisting other healers and learning the specific chants, rites, paintings and songs to bring down the Gods, to save their ill people.

"Miss Bonnie," said Clah, "we will be able to work together and to heal your father. I'm sure of it."

That was all it took for Bonnie. She would do what she had to do, give everything they had, to save her father.

* * *

Dr. Lieber returned the message left by Bonnie Hammer after the receptionist told him that she had called again. He spoke with her but refused to tell her that her father was *already* a patient of his. To do so would have been a breach of confidentiality and also alarming to the daughter. It was well known that Dr. Lieber was a cancer specialist. His patients would be assumed to have cancer. This fact, if the family was unaware, could create chaos for his patient.

To that end, Dr. Lieber worked day and night, seeing patients both in the clinic and in the hospital and then standing at his microscopic and other lab equipment, squinting at tissue samples and body fluids. He used a commercial lab for a lot of the tests, but at the same time he kept up on the latest findings in cancer research and was able to work away at his own theories. True, he was somewhat unorthodox in his clinical practice but the patients that he chose to try to help were in serious shape anyway. Most of them had terminal cancer, already in the later stages when they came to see him. It was a matter of economics and local traditions.

The receptionist buzzed him again and asked him to talk with an Espiritud Soledad. The receptionist briefed him: she was several months pregnant. And she had a tumor growing in her uterus and it was probably keeping pace with the infant in terms of growth. Dr. Lieber was very interested. He had worked with many different kinds of cancer but this sounded like a complex case. Dr. Lieber talked with Espiritud for nearly a half hour. At the end of the conversation he invited her to come to his office as soon as possible. He needed to examine her.

Sprite agreed to come the next day. After all, Tomas was far away in Atlanta. It was her perfect opportunity to have some time to do this on her own. If Dr. Lieber's prognosis was not favorable, she would not even tell Tomas. She wouldn't want him to worry about her.

Chapter 9

Dan Weatherford took seriously Tomas' request to look in on Spirit while he was gone. Even though he had seen her at lunch, Dan dropped by the law office late in the day. He wanted to make sure she was okay but there was another reason to talk with her. The Sheriff had handed Dan another file to work on as he gathered records concerning cancer deaths in the county. The Kingman Brick Company file was not extensive, but had several red tags stuck among the pages. Dan had never seen the file but knew that the Sheriff kept a few politically sensitive files locked in this cabinet. Only he had the key. The Kingman Brick Company was apparently one of those files.

Dan had read enough of the file contents to glaze over with sleepiness. The contents were primarily letters from Cal Kingman going back some thirty years. They thanked Sheriff Andrews for his help with certain legislation or regulations pertaining to mining company. Dan didn't get it. Why would the Sheriff take an interest in talking with politicians at the state capital or the federal agencies? He intended to ask Sprite to take a look at the files and see what she could make of the situation. She would keep the favor in confidence, he trusted.

* * *

Tomas was cruising in the Vanquish at a comfortable 90 mph after too much lunch with Frank. He was already a hundred miles out of Atlanta when the phone rang. It was Frank.

"Hey, buddy."

"What's new?" said Tomas. "Didn't I just see you?"

Frank was serious and didn't respond to Tomas' banter. "I got curious about the famous Dr. Terry Lieber out there in the middle of nowhere..."

"And?"

"The more I thought about him, the more I remembered. I actually met him at a conference in D.C. about five years ago. He was heavily involved in trying to sway Congress about the environmental legislation pending against mining in the Southwest. He gave a session at Johns Hopkins in connection with a trip he had just made to see some of the congressmen about the *situation*, I think he called it. He was impressive, seems to have known who to talk to because it wasn't long after that that some of the states began to tighten up a little on the free-for-all that was mining back then."

"Well, that sounds pretty cool," Tomas said. He wasn't really listening closely, because a traffic box was forming up the road: two semis riding side by side, making it impossible for anyone to pass. And they were going the speed limit, Tomas downshifted with his good hand and watched the needle on the tach drop. The speedometer needle was falling as well.

"Very cool. Especially for someone who might not be a doctor at all."

"Huh?"

"You heard me."

"But..."

"Try checking him out when you get back. You do have Internet service out there, don't you?"

"Of course," Tomas sighed.

"So when I googled his name, I see there he is all right; besides having received about a dozen awards, he is on a more recent list for practicing without a license."

"I'll be damned. He was about to sound to me like the second coming of Christ."

"Well, maybe so. But if he is, he is coming without a license to practice medicine."

"Thanks, Frank, I guess."

"Anytime, buddy. And thanks for lunch."

"Take care of yourself, buddy. And let me know if you hear

anything that I should know about."

Tomas was stuck behind the two massive trucks. He sighed again and rolled his shoulders. The news of Dr. Terry Lieber was interesting. Very interesting indeed. Frank's other news was of concern, but he couldn't worry about that just now.

* * *

Tomas had worked up a head of steam as he crawled behind the big trucks riding in tandem. As soon as he had a wedge opening between them he stomped the accelerator and wiggled around them, like a silver fish. In a flash he outdistanced both trucks as they labored uphill. He noted in his rearview that they had finally aligned themselves so that others could use the passing lane. "Idiots," he muttered. "Learn to drive or say off the road."

The sun turned the tall pine forests of Georgia into a golden maze as Tomas picked up speed and noted the interchanges passing by like pages turned in a book. His mind was on Spirit and he wondered if Dan Weatherford had checked on her that day. He decided to call Spirit. He missed her and there were hundreds of miles between them. The Vanquish was a fast car but it was still only a car. He would have flown back but he needed to begin moving his car collection there if Arizona was to be home for Tomas from now on. He would need a garage to store the exotic car until his home in the hills was done…his mind wandered back and forth between thinking of Spirit and their unborn child, and the logistics of storing the Vanquish. The speedometer crept from ninety to ninety-five.

Tomas found himself humming a Cherokee song that seemed to be lodged permanently in his memory. The words made no sense in English. Translated it would be: *The Bear is very bad, so they say; Long time ago he was bad, so they say; the Bear did so and so, so they say.* In his native tongue it was sung to entertain and please the children, much like the song *Rock a bye, baby.*

Perhaps Tomas was thinking of his unborn child, when the lullaby sprang into his thoughts. He immediately sensed the presence of his mother. She was inextricably linked to the song. Tomas had not been close to his mother in the way that he had been close to his father. She was like background music in the few scenes of his young childhood that he could even recall. Most of his memories began about the time he went to school. At the same age, he began to learn the techniques of farming from his father and grandfather.

But now he remembered that she had called him her *little bear* when he fell down the steps at the farmhouse. *"Little bear,"* she said, *"Be brave, my little bear."* She washed away the tears that started to fall. *"Shh, shh, don't let your father see you cry. Big boys don't cry..."*

Tomas felt tears forming behind his lashes and tried to hold them back. But a few drops insisted and Tomas let them run down the full length of his cheeks before wiping them away with his good hand. He had been strong all during the months of Spirit's difficult pregnancy, but here, alone on a distant highway, he needed the release. The open road was good. The speed of the Vanquish was better; it had been too long since he had the car in his hands. He could listen to the radio but in this part of the country it was hard to find music that he liked. He opted for the music of the highway, the rhythm of the tires hitting the jointed segments of the concrete; the whoosh of wind streaming over the hood and around the side panels.

Tomas reached for his hands free phone and punched in Spirit's cell phone number. She answered on the second ring. Her voice was tired and distracted.

"Hi honey," he said.

"Hi. Sounds like you are in the car. Where are you?" she asked.

"Almost out of Georgia or maybe already in Alabama, I'm not too sure. I have been daydreaming about you, as a matter of fact."

"Oh, well, that's very nice, Tomas. Just don't run off the road, okay?"

"How's the baby?" Tomas asked.

Spirit hesitated. He didn't ask very often about the baby, and she was glad that he was willing to talk about their child. She knew that he had kept an emotional distance in case there was a problem that would have forced a decision about the child. Apparently Tomas had accepted that her decision was made: the child would live no matter what. The "no matter what" part was her life. That possibility was something they didn't discuss.

"The baby is very active today," Spirit said lightly. She loved talking about the baby and imagining what it would look like at this point in the pregnancy. By now the baby was well formed, with fingers and toes and all the other parts. Floating in its' private pool, like a little seahorse.

Tomas kept his eyes on the road as he talked with Spirit. A light rain was beginning to fall and he would need to slow down a little. He was a good driver, but sometimes the weather conditions ruled. "I miss you a lot," he told Spirit.

"I miss you too," she said automatically. The truth was she was enjoying a break from his mothering presence, but there was no way to explain how she just needed a small break from him, without being hurtful.

He detected a ring of falsehood in her tone. He let it go. Tomas knew Spirit well enough to know that even if she didn't miss him today as much as he missed her, she did love him and was as happy as her condition allowed her to be. He admired her courage so much--she was strong and determined to conquer this cancer *and live* and they hoped, have more children in the future.

Spirit changed the subject. "I talked to Ed today about the house," she said. He told me it is coming along fine. The windows are going to be set just like we want them. The view will be magnificent in every season, and yet they will be angled in such a way to make the most of the sun in winter. In the summer the overhang will block the sun's rays at the right time. Oh, and he told me…"

Tomas cut her off, "Did he say that we will be in by Christmas?"

"No," said Spirit.

"Then he had better let me know how many workers he needs to make quicker progress," said Tomas. "I insist that we spend this Christmas in our new home. There will be a tree as tall as those windows. I'll cut it myself if I have to, and drag it in."

Spirit laughed at the image of Tomas trying to set up a ten foot tall spruce, of how big a tree like that would have to be at the base. It would take up the entire family room. They had had this conversation before. When she argued about the size of the tree Tomas would say, "But we need a really big tree to fit all of the presents beneath it."

She knew he was trying hard to stay positive, and to give her something to look forward to just in case--well, just in case. She loved him for that.

"We have time to pick out a Christmas tree. And by the way, since when did you start celebrating the *Christian* holiday? I thought you were an atheist."

"An *agnostic*," Tomas corrected her. "I simply don't give the religious arguments much thought. I'm content to let Mother Nature and Father Time take care of me. But I don't mind borrowing some of the traditions, especially if it means buying you presents, and a little stocking to fill."

"We will have a very confused kid, I think," Spirit said. Then seriously she added, "Tomas, there will be so many things to teach our baby. Sometimes I feel like I still have so much growing up to do. How can I possibly take care of a child and raise it right?"

"Define *right*," Tomas said. "But no, I do know what you mean. For me I've always just done whatever I feel like doing. Selfish, huh?"

"You never had to share, I guess."

"That's no excuse and you know it. Say it: Tomas, you are one selfish man."

"No, I'm not saying that. Look at all you are doing for me. For us."

"Okay, but just so we're clear. I'm not like you, Spirit. I'm not selfless. I don't want to give up everything to help all the poor, abused, victimized people of the world. Not even just our small part of the world."

"What *do* you want out of life, Tomas," Spirit asked. She really wanted to know.

Tomas thought about the question. Then it came to him: he wanted to finish what he had been working on for all his professional years. He wanted to find a cure for cancer. Only before it had been an abstract, an intellectual game and a high staked competition with all of the other doctors and researchers hoping that they would be the one, the hero of the sufferers, the envy of all their associates. Now it was a simple, clear and immediate goal: he wanted to save Spirit's life. Then she might love him as much as he loved her.

"Just you, Spirit," he said.

After they hung up, Tomas concentrated once again on his driving. The light rain had turned to a steady rain. He felt the familiar tightening of his stomach and groin that told him he would need to find a restroom soon. The wet road lay before him like an endless river, as flat as the slow broad rivers that he crossed from time to time as he rode out Alabama. He was on the stretch of highway where he had raced with another driver when he made the long trip from Atlanta to Hidden City in his Ferrari, many months ago. He missed that car, and its smooth ride, but the car was gone--literally gone up in smoke. No need to dwell on those days. Tomas lived in the *now*, not the *then*. He attributed his success to being able to let go of the past and do what needed to be done to come out a winner *today*.

He began to focus his mind on his commitment to finding a cure for Spirit. A plant, his great-grandfather told him through his dream. The answer would be found in a plant. What was it-- the *spirit of the plant would guide him to its healing magic.*

Easy enough for you to say, grandfather, thought Tomas. *But just how am I supposed to find a plant's spirit? What the hell is that supposed to mean?*

Chapter 10

The Arkansas state line greeted Tomas under leaden skies and a stinking barrier of garbage. It looked like someone with a grudge against the entire state had bulldozed the contents of a city dump right up to the state line. Tomas didn't need to slow down to gape at the line of torn trash bags, used disposable diapers, water bottles, smeared fast food bags and other reeking waste pushed up against a tree line. The garbage fence was long enough that he could study even at seventy miles per hour.

"What the hell?" he muttered.

The radio was tuned to a Little Rock talk show. For an hour Tomas tried to catch a weather report as the light rain became heavier in short bursts, then slacked off. But the skies grew increasingly dark. The clouds to the west now showed thick patches of green tinged with pink and purple. The radio was useless; all he was getting was static interspersed with someone ranting about the World Bank. He couldn't be bothered. He pressed the tuner control until a weather report came through. More rain expected in the Little Rock area, now showing signs of flash floods in the low lying areas.

Tomas was taken back to his last trip from Atlanta to Hidden City. That hail storm in northeast Texas had destroyed his Ferrari. He'd be damned if he would damage another car. Rain wouldn't hurt him, but the clouds in the west looked worrisome. A long, vertical bolt of lightning split the western horizon, followed shortly by thunder. Out of habit he measured the distance by counting the seconds between the flash of lightning and the thunder, counting off one Mississippi, two Mississippi, three Mississippi, between the sight and sound. The lightning was three miles away. Straight ahead. There was no way of avoiding this storm.

Tomas groaned. He knew that Arkansas had been hit with a lot of rain this past season. There had been serious flooding. He looked closely at the landscape to check for signs of recent flooding, like flattened grass and gullies washed out of the hillsides, leaving red silt deltas where the gully flattened out to meet the road. What he saw was no comfort. It looked like the area had seen a lot of rain recently. The creeks he crossed were full: the water roiled just a foot or two beneath the low bridges.

The storms that had passed through held a lot of wind. There were medium sized pines that were twisted by the wind with such force that the trunks splintered and the top halves of the trees fell in sharp angles. Tomas guessed from the freshly splintered trunks of the trees still standing that the storm damage was less than a week old.

He rounded a curve at 70 miles per hour. Ahead he saw a car pulled off on the shoulder of the road. A woman paced beside it, holding a cell phone in one hand. He slowed and took in the woman: about thirty years old, dark hair, and dressed up in what looked like business clothes. He slowed to check out the late 1990s Jeep Cherokee. The tires were intact; he would not have to change a tire if he chose to help her. Tomas pulled over ahead of her car and put the Vanquish in neutral. The woman saw him get out of the car and began to walk toward him. She said something into the phone and then snapped it shut, but kept it in her palm. She looked at the sky and pushed her damp hair off of her forehead.

She looked at Tomas and his car and decided he was probably just stopping to help her out. Still, she kept a distance when she called out to him. "Thanks for stopping," she said, "I pulled off the road to try to figure out what to do. Now it won't start. I'm worried about the rain. There was flooding over in the next county yesterday."

"So-o-o-o-o, you're from around here, then."

"I used to be. I'm here visiting my folks. And trying to do

some business at the same time. I work out of Little Rock."

"You looked a little bit too dressed up to be here on a fishing trip."

She laughed. He noticed how pretty she was when she did that. Her face lost its tense look. He recognized that look from his go-go days in Atlanta, He guessed that she was in sales of some kind. She was used to talking with people, and good at it.

Tomas looked at the Jeep. "I know a little about cars," he said. "Shall I take a look at it while you're waiting to be rescued?"

She was eying the Vanquish. "Sure, thanks," she said. "That's a great car. What's it?"

"That's an Aston Martin Vanquish."

"I've never seen one of those."

Tomas began to walk toward the Jeep. "Do you want to give me the keys?"

She handed them over, then thrust out her hand to meet his. "I'm Casey Baldwin."

He solemnly shook her hand. "I'm Tomas Hotone."

"That's a different name - - Hotone...are you from around here?"

"No, just passing through. Hotone is a Cherokee name. People are never sure how to pronounce it. It is spelled H-O-T-O-NE- like Hot One."

She looked at him out of the corner of her eyes. "And are you?" she asked teasingly.

Tomas couldn't help himself. "Sometimes," he said.

She fell silent. They were at the car and Tomas stepped in, keying the ignition. The Cherokee didn't respond.

He tried again. Nothing at all.

"When was the last time you replaced the battery in this thing?" Tomas said.

She looked at him blankly. "Never."

"Well there you have it," said Tomas. "You know, batteries don't last forever. You have to change them."

Casey was looking at the toe of her shoe. "There isn't

anyone coming to rescue me."

Thunder rolled in the horizon. The boom reverberated and grew dull.

Tomas and Casey both looked at the sky at the same time. They looked anywhere but at each other. There was electricity and the smell of ozone in the air.

Tomas determined to play the gentleman. "I could take you someplace," he said. I don't know the area, but if you do, I'll take you to a parts store for a battery, bring you back and help you put it in."

Casey relaxed and smiled up at him. "I'd really appreciate that," she said.

Tomas glanced at his watch. It was almost 4:00. Any parts store would be closed in an hour or two.

"We had better hit the road," he said. Just then a fat raindrop hit the red soil at his foot, causing a small divot. Then another. And another. They looked and could see the wind pick up. It blew the smaller trees in a circular pattern. Larger branches started to stir.

"Hurry," Tomas called to Casey. "Let's get to my car."

"I need to grab my bag out of the car. I don't want to leave my laptop in the car in the middle of nowhere." She was already headed back to the Cherokee.

* * *

The storm blew in a fury. The saturated red rock stream beds sluiced the torrents down ditches in a rusty gush. Tomas drove without seeing more than ten feet in front of the car. There was scarce traffic.

"I can't tell you how much I appreciate your help,"

"Where is the nearest town?" asked Tomas.

"I'd say about five miles away."

"Just keep going and there will be an exit there?"

"That's what I remember. It has been a while since I drove around here. Things have changed."

"So what kind of work do you do?" asked Tomas.

"I'm a mortgage broker."

This was something that Tomas knew about. Some of his portfolio was in hedge funds made up of mortgage investments. They were looking good too. "How is business?" he asked.

"Couldn't be better, I guess. I'm closing at least ten loans a month right now."

"Compared to--what?"

"Last year at this time it was only about half that."

"Well that sounds great. Good for you, and good for the people who are getting loans and buying homes. It's a win-win situation, don't you think?"

"That's what the managers tell us."

"But?"

She looked at him and smiled. "But nothing. Trade secret, anyway."

Tomas' business brain was clicking. "Come on, give it up. What's going on out there?"

Casey stifled a yawn. She was far more concerned with getting her car fixed and getting home out of this rain, to be worried about mortgages. But she could see he wasn't giving up.

"Some people get loans who really can't afford them. Last year I couldn't have gotten them approved. Now, it's like the big lenders are handing out money to most anyone. And the lending terms are so convoluted that the people don't know what they are signing. Their lawyers just let it slide."

Tomas shrugged. He had been around long enough to know that everything in business has a cycle, ups and downs. Nothing to worry about; normal stuff. But the talk of business was keeping his mind off other thoughts about this woman.

Casey was in good spirits now. She liked this guy and she liked his car. He wasn't trying to make moves on her, at least not yet. If anything, she was thinking about making some moves on him. That was a turn-on, too. Usually the men she met took things as far as they could, as soon as they could. It was a relief to be with someone who was more...mature.

Tomas fell silent and tried to think of something more to say. The rainstorm was not relenting; if anything, it rained harder. The wind died down but the rain clouds hung above spilling more and more water onto the saturated fields and filled waterways. He almost missed the sign for the exit but veered across the traffic lanes at the last minute to make it onto the ramp.

Ten minutes later Tomas and Casey ran from the Vanquish through a Walmart store parking lot. The sewers were so full that they were backing up and spouted water like so many fountains around the perimeter of the store. By the time they were inside their shoes were soaked through. Tomas picked out the right battery for Casey's Jeep. She located a rack of umbrellas and bought the biggest one she could. They hurried back to the Vanquish and plowed water as they crossed the shallow pond of parking lot.

Casey's hair dried in ringlets as they drove back to the Interstate and finally reached the spot where she left her Jeep. Neither one of them noticed that there was no way to get across to the side of the Interstate; there was no crossroad. Tomas considered just driving across the median on the grass, but he could see standing water in the wide ditch and wasn't sure he could make it across without getting stuck.

Casey looked forlornly at her Jeep. She thought that she saw water all around its' wheels as they passed it by and continued driving in the opposite direction. The water by now was gathering force in its run down the hillsides and across the pavement so that the Vanquish left a spew of wake behind it. At least they were going uphill.

Tomas continued driving. Where is the freaking exit? thought Tomas. He noticed a state patrol car approaching them in the westbound lanes with its lights flashing. Later, a fire truck bore down, its siren a thin wail in the pouring rain.

The next exit came up more than ten miles past the point where the Jeep was pulled over. Tomas and Casey were relieved they were finally headed in the right direction. But as they started to turn back onto the westbound entrance ramp a state police car blocked the road. The officer was outside his car, wearing a thick plastic orange cover on his hat and a fluorescent poncho. He waved them down to a stop with his heavy flashlight.

Tomas slowed and pulled up to the officer. He punched a button and the driver side window went down a couple of inches. The officer leaned over and pointed his flashlight at Tomas. "I'm sorry, sir, this road is closed. There's standing water a little further down."

Casey looked past Tomas to the patrolman. "But, Officer, that's my Jeep down the road. The battery went dead and we had to go get another one…"

"I'm sorry ma'am," he said firmly. "The road is closed. You'll have to come back when it reopens. Call the state police road conditions number before you try again, though. It looks like we're in for a lot of weather for the next day or so."

Tomas ran his broad hand over his short cropped hair. *Now what,* he thought.

He looked over at Casey and saw tears beginning to form in her dark green eyes.

Tomas sighed. He was stuck and he knew it. He couldn't just leave her out here, he would have to be the Good Samaritan. Maybe it would stop raining soon and the water would subside. They would just pop the battery in and the Jeep would fire up and she would be on her way.

It would be as easy as that.

Chapter 11

Dr. Terry Lieber consulted his appointment schedule and saw that it was going to be another hectic day. He was scheduled to be in Scottsdale for a noon luncheon to deliver a speech. His topic was "The Relative Efficacy of Oral Chelation Treatment Compared to Delivery by Intravenous Infusion" for the American Chelating Therapy Center.

The non-profit center was gaining members every day as people became increasingly concerned with the effects of heavy metals in the human body. Although the organization had been around since the 1970's, recent years had seen a bump up in numbers as the frequency of autism in children exploded, and some parents blamed the children's early immunizations for causing autism.

Dr. Lieber chose to drive. He had always hated flying. The events of September 11th had not helped his attitude.

If he left early and encountered no traffic snarls he could get to Scottsdale, deliver his speech, and be back at this clinic to see one of his current patients, Jim Hammer as well as a new patient. He was keenly interested in how Jim was doing. The man's cancer, once discovered, had progressed unrelentingly. Dr. Lieber was considering a radical move.

During his drive, Dr. Lieber rehearsed his speech. Most of it was rote; he had been advocating the use of chelation therapy for most of his professional life. He had spoken at over sixty conferences across the country and had testified before congress on multiple occasions. Chelation therapy was outside the usual treatments for illnesses even though Dr. Lieber and other proponents believed it to be safe and sensible when done correctly. The physicians who were opponents of the therapy believed it to be less effective than other mainstream treatments, and possibly quite dangerous.

The patients wanted as many toxins out as possible. Dr. Lieber was happy to help. He touted the chelation process wherever he could. Today he would be preaching to the choir; the annual meeting was always well attended by similar minded physicians, as well as chiropractors, alternative medicine providers, massage therapists, and a wide range of ill people.

* * *

After the vegetarian luncheon the President of the Chelation Therapy Center, Lillian Tarnower, introduced Dr. Lieber. "You have all heard of this man, Dr. Terry Lieber. He has toiled in the vineyards of progressive medical treatment for cancer, heart disease and other evils of our times without seeking fame or wealth for himself. We're fortunate to have this fighter with us today, one who is as comfortable speaking out to a group of congressmen against unsafe mining techniques as he is comforting a terminally ill child. I give you...Dr. Terry Lieber."

Applause burst forth from the conference attendees. The noise level rose and then died away and people poured themselves one more cup of coffee from stainless steel pitchers and settled in for the keynote speaker.

Dr. Lieber rose from the head table and stepped to the podium.

"Good afternoon everyone and thank you for attending this conference. You are all soldiers in the ongoing battle to create respect for a procedure we call Chelation Therapy. For those of you who are brand new to this arena, and perhaps here to gain information on a possible treatment for you or a loved one, I will give you a brief overview of the procedures, the recent breakthroughs in chelation, and a prediction as to where this technique will take us in the future.

Those of you old enough to remember the 1970s and 80s may remember that some health conscious people elected to have the silver fillings removed from their teeth. They were convinced that the fillings were leaking toxic heavy metals into their bodies, and that the toxins were making them feel sick. They reported muscle aches and pains, weakness, nausea, dizziness, mental confusion, and more.

Mainstream consumers laughed at us or ignored us. We who saw the logical connection went further than just having fillings removed, or using high colonics to flush out other pollutants in our bodies, we entered into Chelation Therapy.

The process and concept is not difficult. Imagine if you will a substance that will find heavy metals in the body, attach itself to the metal molecules, and stay attached to form clumps that are then filtered through livers and intestine and kidneys--and simply excreted from the body like any other waste. In this way the patient rids themselves of dangerous pollutants. People report rapid improvement--even recovery--from debilitating illness once the poisons are out of their systems. They have more energy, headaches disappear, muscle function improves and they can think more clearly.

Now that's not a bad payoff for the cost of the supplements needed. The active ingredient--the substance that finds and captures the heavy metals in our bloodstreams--is known as EDTA. The oral tablets used by thousands of people may not be potent enough for everyone, depending on their size, and the severity of the toxicity in that patient's system. For those cases, or if the patient simply opts for this treatment, there is intravenous delivery of the EDTA. The biggest objection to intravenous delivery of EDTA is that the rate of infusion--the speed of the IV delivery, you could say--must be carefully controlled. The procedures are slow and the gradual infusion must be measured precisely if the patient is to have optimal result. A qualified therapist can easily monitor and control the rate of flow for the correct dosage.

Dr. Lieber pushed his glasses up and rested both palms on the podium. He looked into the eyes of the crowd, and drew quiet for a moment. It was the art of the pause.

He began again, louder now, and more syncopated.

"People, it is time to call for the right to have chelation therapy covered by insurance, just as it would be for radiation therapy, or chemotherapy. Now I'm not going so far out on a limb as to say that these two standard treatments for cancer should not be used. But I believe that a patient should have a real choice. And that those who choose to use chelation therapy should be able to choose their treatment. The use of chemotherapy and radiation increase the toxic burden to the individuals who are assigned those treatments. Those who truly believe that it was toxic elements that jump-started their disease in the first place are naturally reluctant to add to the load. I respect that. I consider it part of my professional duty to participate in the solutions in a number of ways. First of all, as many of you know, I have been a watchdog of industry--especially the mining industry--and have gone to Washington, D.C. and the state capitol on many occasions to give my testimony as to the probable cancer effects of exposure to toxic substances in the workplace. Right now a major offender, the Kingman Brick Company, is engaged in providing information to the environmental agency within the state, to explain the cancer cluster that seems to be emerging among former Kingman employees. These people inhaled tiny radioactive particles of something called thorium.

Thorium is a radioactive substance that occurs naturally in soils, especially in conjunction with the earth and gravel used in the manufacture of home building bricks. Thorium is linked to several different cancers, but most often thought to be the cause of a type of leukemia and also liver cancer. This just happens to be the kind of cancers found in a group of middle aged and older men who worked at Kingman in the past. A coincidence? I...don't...think...so.

The men, and women, who have died in recent years in the area where I practice, are not wealthy people. Many have other health problems, and most no longer have any insurance benefits. Some have begun taking over-the-counter supplements on their own in a desperate attempt to get some benefit. In my opinion they may as well not waste their money. The drug store supplements are not tested or regulated and may do more harm than good. Self-medication is not a good option.

The future of intravenous infusion in chelation therapy holds great promise. Perhaps you are not aware that chelation is now the subject of experimental studies for the prevention of heart disease. The EDTA works as well on binding with arterial plaque as it does on heavy metals: mercury, zinc, cadmium, and the list goes on. Wouldn't it be wonderful if EDTA chelation therapy could replace heart by-pass surgery? The risk of infection, a common killer of those who have undergone successful bypass surgery only to die of a bacterial infection, is minimized. The problem is that the EDTA may be too good at binding with needed substances like calcium, and removing it from the body at an unhealthy rate. So the procedures must be carefully monitored, and supported with research grants so that we may reap the benefits of chelating therapy.

I'm pleased to take any questions or comments that you may wish to offer. Please stand and ask your question so that everyone can hear you. Yes? You, third row..."

* * *

Dr. Lieber was eager to get back on the road. Following any speaking engagement Dr. Lieber was sure to get one or two calls from someone ill with cancer, or a relative of a cancer victim. They would be willing to drive any distance, even out into the desert to Dr. Lieber's remote clinic, for the hope of a pardon from the illness.

Dr. Lieber's patient, Jim Hammer, was a case in point. A former alcoholic, now a devout AA member, would give everything he had to beat his cancer. He had not yet told his wife or grown daughter of the seriousness of his condition. He had little time left, in Dr. Lieber's view. Without aggressive treatment, he would die soon. Even with aggressive treatment his chances of recovery or even remission were slim. And yet he was still young enough and his body was still strong enough--Dr. Lieber hoped--to withstand the chelation therapy that Dr. Lieber had been giving him. The patient was unaware of what Dr.

Lieber was doing--he thought that he was being giving antibiotics or vitamin supplements, or both. They didn't talk about the treatments. Jim was not a talkative man and asked few questions. He put his faith in Dr. Lieber and in the doctor's superior knowledge, just like all the other men and the two women who Dr. Lieber had used in his chelation research.

The miles rolled by. Flat desert flowed into hillier terrain. Saguaro cactus fields gave way to birch and aspen forests, and the red rock canyons deepened. He was running later than he liked; Jim would be waiting. And then there was that new patient to see.

* * *

By the time Dr. Lieber arrived at his clinic, it was growing dark. Both Jim and the new patient--a hugely pregnant young woman--were waiting for him. The two seemed to know each other; the woman was asking Jim about his wife, Clara, and his daughter, Bonnie. Dr. Lieber excused himself for being late, and ushered Jim into his first patient room.

The two men shook hands, and Dr. Lieber observed that Jim's hand was growing thinner with every visit. Dr. Lieber patted Jim's bony shoulder. Quickly Dr. Lieber positioned Jim in the recliner. He left the room momentarily, and returned with an IV and a plastic bag containing his solution. In moments the fluid was dripping into Jim's vein.

Jim lay back with his eyes closed. His face was slack, resigned. He was weary of the treatment, but he believed in Dr. Lieber.

Dr. Lieber glanced at the clock and saw he needed to hurry. He knew that he shouldn't: the rate of infusion in the procedure was important. But a part of him was curious and wanted to push the envelope. To get closer to knowing exactly the point at which too fast was too fast. This was something that should be known to the scientific community and to the practitioners. It needed to be measured, and documented, and made known to others who were now just guesstimating the danger point.

Dr. Lieber looked again at the exhausted patient. The doctor reached for the IV equipment and with a practiced hand, opened the valve. He watched as the bubbles in the bag began to move faster, and faster.

* * *

In the waiting room, Sprite was getting impatient. She understood that delays happened, and that each patient had to wait his or her turn, but she was getting tired and cross. She was the only one in the waiting room and even the nurse-receptionist had gone home long ago. Finally, Dr. Lieber appeared. She stood up and shook his hand. He pointed her in the direction of the second examining room.

Sprite settled into a straight backed plastic chair. The doctor sat at a small writing desk near her and studied her face. He saw the alert intelligence of her eyes. He estimated that she was at least eight months pregnant.

"What brings you here, Espiritud?" Dr. Lieber asked Sprite. He had read her legal name on the file.

"Two things, really. And please, call me Sprite. Everyone else does."

Dr. Lieber smiled. "Okay, Sprite. What can I do for you?"

"Two things," she said tersely.

"I'm a lawyer investigating a situation. I am looking into what seems to be a cluster of cancer deaths in the area over the past few years. Your name was on the death certificates of most of the people who have died. Deputy Dan Weatherford of the Waipiti County Sheriff's office is working on this and I don't know too many details yet. A brick factory over the state line has also asked us to get some information. Apparently the state and maybe the federal environmental protection agencies are working with…"

"Kingman Brick Company," he said, finishing her sentence for her. "Yes, I do know a lot about that situation. And I have treated a lot of men and I think, two women, who had worked at Kingman's company back in the sixties and seventies. In my opinion, there was a definite link between the dust they breathed while working there, and the cancers they developed. I have testified before about my opinions, both at the statehouse and in Washington. But the real problem, in my opinion, is that there has been resistance to doing anything to correct the situation at Kingman, and at some other mining operations."

"But everything is regulated now, isn't it?"

"Finally, yes. In theory. I don't want to say too much, you see, but for years in this area, the mining industry was in charge. Mining was just too important, and I believe that a lot of money and well, *favors*, were provided to lawmakers to protect the mining industries. You know how it works, the campaign contributions, the dinners at fancy restaurants. I could give you an example of how long it took for a strong bill to pass in congress---but of course I have no hard proof--only what I've heard and what makes sense to me."

Sprite nodded her head. "Yes, I do know how these things go. When money is at stake, when one's business is on the line, people will do desperate things."

Dr. Lieber agreed. "We can talk all night about that, but you said there was another reason that you are here?"

Sprite's face tensed. "Yes, Obviously, I'm pregnant. During one of the routine blood tests, something showed up that made my doctor do some additional testing, Then CT scans and the like. There is a mass growing right up close to the baby. A tumor of some kind."

Dr. Lieber frowned. This is something he didn't normally encounter. "And your obstetrician recommended that you have a biopsy?"

"That and more. There was talk of surgery. I refused because they said they could not guarantee that I would not lose the baby. "

"But your life could be at risk,"

"I made the decision," she said, "to carry the baby to term."

"I'll need to run more tests, if you wish me to treat you."

"I should tell you that my husband is also a cancer researcher. I get the feeling that he knows more than he is telling me. That he is hiding something from me. That's why I'm here. I want you to tell me the truth about my situation. No sugar-coating, okay?"

"Okay. Fair enough. If you will excuse me for a moment, I need to check on another patient."

"Of course."

Dr. Lieber opened the door of Room One and found that Jim's IV was signaling as completed. Jim seemed to be the same; he had tolerated the procedure just fine. Dr. Lieber scheduled the next appointment, in another two weeks. Jim hesitated. Dr. Lieber arched his eyebrows and looked at Jim, saying, "Is that a problem?"

Jim started to tell him that he would have just finished with his sand painting healing with Hosteen Clah III. Then he thought better of it. He would be recovered from the effort of the healing by the time of the next appointment. "No, that would be fine," he said.

Jim felt lightheaded and wobbly as he left the treatment room. Each day now, he felt a little worse.

Sprite waited patiently for Dr. Lieber's return. She knew that she had to decide if she wanted to become his patient. She liked the man's demeanor and had heard nothing but good about him from the families on the Reservation. She liked his activism in taking on the mining companies; that was not an easy thing to do. Still, he had not yet examined her or offered an opinion. She would bring her records to this clinic soon. What would Tomas think about that?

Chapter 12

Sprite stopped by her office with a heavy heart. She faxed Dr. Lieber the CT scans and lab reports and sonograms performed previously. She still suspected Tomas had been filtering the information that she received--with the best intentions of course--to protect her and to keep the stress from doing additional harm. But it was her body. And she had a right to know that outweighed Tomas' decision to put a spin on the test findings. She was angry. And she was afraid in a way that she had never been afraid before.

She drove along the two-lane hardtop back to Hidden City. She knew that Tomas was delayed somewhere in Arkansas due to flooding, so there was no pressing reason to go home except for her bulldog's need for her nightly walk.

Sprite was glad that Tomas would not be home tonight. It gave her the space to think about all that Dr. Lieber had said. She pictured the race going on inside her: the baby growing larger and stronger, needing all that she had to give to develop in a healthy way, and the shadowy tumor also growing larger being supported by her body against her will. One thing was certain; there was not much time left for speculation. She wanted most of all to give her baby its best chance for a healthy birth. That meant waiting--doing nothing except keeping busy and planning the house that would be the child's home.

Suddenly she wanted to see their home in Desert View more than anything. She would not be able to drive there that night, but with Tomas gone she could go tomorrow. She would call Ed and make sure that he would be there working. She could get up early, before the sunrise, and drive in the cool gray hush of the predawn desert. She could stop in to check on the Hammer family. She would not worry about the medical opinions just now.

Sprite pulled in to the Coop for a late night snack. She had not eaten much dinner and was starting to feel dizzy and weak. Nick was glad to see her. The new waitress took her order and then attempted some polite small talk.

"How's it going?" she asked.

Sprite sat down heavily at a table for four. She was glad there were only a few people in the restaurant. As she looked around she noticed a dark man with a lined face. He wore a soft hat with a wide brim and a number of bird feathers tucked into the hat band. The hat rested on his back and was tethered to the man with a thin leather strap. From the strap hung metal charms, beads and chunks of hollowed bone. He was slowly eating a bowl of clear soup. He looked up when Sprite sat down across the narrow aisle and nodded to her.

Hosteen Clah III recognized the young lawyer. He had heard that she was pregnant from Bonnie, but that there was a problem. He gazed at Sprite and took the measure of her weighty midsection with his dark eyes. When he lifted his eyes to her face, he met her gaze. He noticed the tears welling up in her eyes.

When the healer finished his broth--it was all that he had eaten on this final day before the complete fast--he rose and walked quietly to Sprite's table. "I'm Hosteen Clah III," he said. Sprite looked directly into his eyes. She felt something when she looked at this man; and now she knew why. She had heard of his healing powers and knew the legend of his grandfather, or was it great-grandfather?

Sprite bowed her head and spoke softly. "It's my great honor to meet you. Please forgive me for not recognizing you immediately. Naturally I've heard of you and your gifts."

"I've also heard of you, and if I may say, your gifts as well."

Sprite looked up in confusion. "What do you mean? I'm no

healer."

The healer smiled and put his hand on the top of Sprite's head. "Why of course you are. I have heard many stories of your visits to the families on the Reservation. For many years you've worked to help the families there. I know that you take milk to the children. I know the people call you *Weeping Eye* because you care so much."

"I'll soon have my own child to take care of," said Sprite. "If all goes well."

"We have a friend in common," said Hosteen.

"Yes, I think you are talking about Jim Hammer, and Clara and Bonnie. They've been talking about you while they're getting ready for the sand painting healing."

"Yes, it will be soon. Will you come?"

"I'd like to go but I'm not sure. Ever since I heard about it I've been thinking about you. And now that I've met you, I would like to go even more."

"If I may ask, are you all right? Is everything going well with the baby?"

"Not exactly."

"I've heard talk that there's a problem."

"Yes. In fact, I visited a new doctor tonight. Even though my husband is a cancer researcher. I wanted a second opinion from Dr. Lieber. Do you know who he is?"

The healer was quiet for a moment, as if wanting to tell her something, but then decided against it. "Yes, I'm aware of him. I don't understand all of his techniques, I confess. But I've worked with many of the people who he has treated."

"He seems dedicated to helping the people here. I respect that."

"The people that I have talked with about him don't doubt his sincerity."

Sprite was sensitive to the phrasing. "But?"

Hosteen Clah III again grew quiet. "I'm not sure that Dr. Lieber respects our ways. My ways."

"My husband is also very knowledgeable about cancer. But

he has not treated patients for several years now. He was working on a research project, trying to find a cure, as well as being a surgeon, when he had a mild stroke."

"And? Did he find a cure?"

"No, I'm afraid that there was an interruption while he was trying to recover from his own illness. And then he found me, and has been living here in Hidden City for over a year now. We married and now we will have this child."

"Why does that make you sad?"

Sprite looked down at her belly. Even though the diner was virtually empty, she didn't feel comfortable talking to the healer, not here and not tonight.

"Do you think we could talk about this another time--soon, I hope. I'm just feeling a bit tired right now."

"Of course. Will you come to Jim's healing?"

Sprite decided that she would. "Your invitation is irresistible," she said.

Hosteen tipped his hat. "I won't be able to speak with you during the chant. But I'll know that you're there. Perhaps when it's done you will permit me the honor of helping you with your…condition."

Just being near the man was helping Sprite to relax. She had considered the native medicine, but Tomas was skeptical. He was not one to disparage the old ways, especially when his own great grandfather had been such a powerful healer, but when it came to Spirit's treatment, he couldn't afford to take chances. He was trained in Western medicine.

The healer walked slowly but purposefully out of the dining room. He didn't look back at her.

Spirit was suddenly lonely for Tomas, and decided to call him when she got back to the trailer. She wasn't sure if she would tell him about her visit to Dr. Lieber, but she would tell him about this encounter with the famous Hosteen Clah III.

* * *

Sprite reached her trailer and hauled herself through the doorway and into the sitting area. She glanced at the clock and saw that it was later than she thought. She had better call Ed at the construction site before she called Tomas.

Ed picked up on the third ring. "Hello, Spirit," he said. He had seen the number on the display screen on his cell phone.

"Hi Ed," Spirit said, "I'm thinking about driving up to see the house tomorrow. Tomas is out of town and I need a change of scenery. Will you be there tomorrow?"

Ed knew that she knew the answer; Tomas had hired him to work exclusively on the house until it was done. Ed was living in Tomas' big RV at the site to save the time of traveling to Desert View every day. "You bet, ma'am," he said.

"Will I be in your way if I come up tomorrow?"

"No, no, of course not," Ed said. "I'll need to move some of the saws out of your way, that's all. We're done with the wiring and framing, and the inspector was out here already to inspect the electric work. Everything is fine. We're dry walling now. I'm not promising you will be all done by Christmas, but I'm working toward that."

"I can hardly wait to see it. You know how much we appreciate your work."

"The last thing to go in will be the sinks and countertop. Then we will stain and finish all the woodwork, then inside paint, carpeting, and your appliances. Everything is falling into place.

"Tomas is bringing back one of his cars from Atlanta. He will probably want to park it in the garage as soon as possible. God forbid he should have it out in the weather."

"Yeah, I know it's coming out here. I've been talking with Tomas about every day."

"I'm going to call him right now, to let him know that I'm going up to see the house tomorrow. You'll let me know if you need me to bring anything to you?"

"I can't think of anything right now. You be careful now. Are you feeling okay?"

Sprite sighed but decided to keep her mood to herself. "I'll be fine, Ed. Thanks for asking."

Sprite placed a call to Tomas' cell phone number. It rang five or six times before a female voice answered. Sprite mumbled apologies for dialing a wrong number, then hung up. I must be more tired than I thought," she thought. She punched in the numbers slower this time, watching the LCD display the familiar number.

Again, a female voice answered. No wrong number, no mistake, a woman was answering Tomas cell phone, this late at night. Sprite didn't know what to think. The memory of a night long ago, when she had called Tomas at his Atlanta apartment and a woman had answered the telephone there, tugged at her heart. She had not spoken to Tomas for several years after that incident. But that was then, this was now. They were married now. She was having his baby, their baby. Tears that had been trying to spill ever since she left Dr. Lieber's office began to stream down her cheeks. Get a grip, she told herself.

"I'm trying to reach Tomas Hotone," Spirit said, her voice choking just enough to be heard by the woman holding the cell phone.

"Oh he is in the motel office," the woman said cheerfully. "Shall I give him a message?"

"No," said Sprite, "Please don't."

Chapter 13

Tomas returned to the Vanquish with two motel keys in his hand. He handed one to Casey as he ducked into the car. "Here you are," he said. "You are in room 362." It was still raining heavily and Tomas shoulders and hair were soaked through in only the time it took to hurry from the motel office door to the car.

"Thank you," Casey said. "I'll pay you back, I promise. I wasn't expecting to be stranded out here, with my credit cards locked into the glove compartment, and not able to get to my car."

Tomas shrugged. "I know what you mean. The last time I came through here, it was as dry as dust. One of the worst droughts that Arkansas has ever seen. When I got to Texas, I got caught in a hailstorm that destroyed my Ferrari. This time, I'll be lucky if the Vanquish doesn't float away. He looked at Casey and shook his head. "I guess it's a good thing that I'm an old farm boy. I'm used to changeable weather. We'll just hole up here and hope that when the rain stops and when the water goes down on the roads, you still have a car."

Casey's eyes widened. "What if I don't?" she asked.

"Then I hope you have good insurance."

Casey laughed.

And Tomas noticed again how good she looked, how easy it might be, so far away from home, to spend a sweet evening together with this pretty woman. But he was in control of himself and wasn't worried about letting a chance meeting develop into anything more complicated. It wouldn't be worth it--couldn't be worth risking the second chance he had been given to make a life with Spirit.

Casey was looking straight ahead now, through the windshield, at the water cascading down the glass. The air in the car was growing close. She noticed Tomas looking at her and said, "What are you thinking about?"

Tomas hesitated and then said, "You."

"What about me?"

"How easy it would be to enjoy the evening. You know, a nice dinner, a bottle of wine…."

"I should tell you that I'm engaged."

"I already noticed the ring."

"In fact, I should call him and let him know that I'm all right."

"Of course."

"And what about you? Is there a someone somewhere waiting for you?"

Tomas shut his eyes. He could see Spirit moving awkwardly through the trailer, putting away the dishes, and watching the news on the tiny television that dangled from a bracket in the sitting area. "Yes," he said, "there is someone."

"Is she expecting you tonight?"

"No, not until tomorrow night. She is in Arizona."

"So you have a girlfriend?"

Tomas placed his hand on her shoulder. As much as he wanted to avoid touching her, his hand was drawn to her like it had a life of its own. "She's my wife."

"I don't see any wedding ring."

Tomas pulled a thin gold chain from beneath his pullover shirt. A plain gold ring dangled from it. He held it up and it swung slightly, as if trying to find balance. "I wear this. My ring finger is damaged."

"A likely story," she teased. "Doesn't your wife mind?"

"I've never given her reason to be worried."

"And yet you seem to be very attracted to me."

"Oh, I am, definitely, I am. I apologize for my testosterone. Really, I do."

She laughed again. "Please," she said, "Let's not do anything that either one of us will have to lie about later on, okay?"

Tomas appreciated her good sense. He had been close to losing his own, and she had rescued him.

Suddenly the rain stopped. On the count of three, they bolted for the door to the motel.

* * *

Spirit paced the length of the trailer, crying and trying to make sense of what the woman's voice on the telephone had said. Tomas wasn't there; he was in the motel office. There was only one reason that a person would be in a motel office, in her experience. He was getting a room, the bastard.

She made herself go to bed, but once in bed she couldn't sleep. No position was comfortable. She could feel the baby's heel--or some insistent part-- pushing into her lower rib. She found it difficult to breathe with the weight of the child on her when she tried to lie on her back. Sleeping on her stomach was out of the question. She rolled from side to side, hurting inside and out. Her telephone rang, but she ignored it. There was no one in the world that she wanted to talk to just then. Bitterness rose in her throat as sour as bile. She unplugged the house phone and shut off her cell phone.

An hour went by, then two. Sprite gave up on sleep. She stepped outside the trailer and looked up at the clear, star-scattered night sky. The moon was full and the air held a cold freshness that promised cooler days now that October was drawing to an end. She drank in the air like water. Returning inside the trailer, she put on the tea kettle and sat in her reading chair.

On the table was the file folder that Dan Weatherford had brought to her concerning the Kingman Brick Company. What was it he asked her to do? Her mind was increasingly foggy lately, though the doctor told her that was common in pregnancy and most likely had to do with fatigue. She was advised to rest often and get a full night's sleep every night.

"Yeah, right," muttered Spirit.

To keep her mind from obsessing about Tomas she picked up the Kingman file. Silently she began to read. There were many letters in the file from Cal Kingman, the owner of the company, to Sheriff Andrews. There was a brief, but courteous, response to each letter. The exchanges went back almost twenty years. Taken individually, the thank you notes from the Kingman Company and the cryptic notes sent back seemed innocent. Grouped together, the exchanges seemed odd: it was more like reading telegraphed messages written in some kind of code. But why?

Sprite read through the letters again, and again. Her old remedy for emotional hurt--to distract herself with her work--helped her to pass the time. The more she read them, the stranger they seemed. No one would have written essentially the same "thank you" notes, almost down to the same words and phrases, over such a long period of time. It was not usual to reply in the same way to a thank you note: no one wrote a thank you note to acknowledge a thank you note. Certainly a man would never do such a thing. She made a note to call Dan Weatherford in the morning.

She was still reading the stilted language of the letters, when weariness gained the upper hand. She fell asleep in her reading chair, a cold cup of tea on the table beside her, just as the moon began to set behind the distant mesas.

* * *

Sheriff Hank Andrews was having a sleepless night himself. He had been suffering from intermittent headaches, and leg cramps, for several days. Leg pain was an old enemy to him. He had fought the aching with salves and heating pads and aspirin, whiskey and hot baths, for too long to recall. But tonight was different. It was as if his legs were held in a vise that was gradually being tightened. Muscle spasms wracked his calves.

Hank lived alone; his wife had left him long ago for a salesman who lived next door to the couple. At the time Hank was so busy with politics that he barely noticed that his wife spent hours and hours out of the house. She claimed to be gardening, but Hank, if he had paid any attention, would have seen that the number of weeds in the flower beds never declined

When people asked about her absence at a political function, he just said that she was at home--just not at his home. The men laughed harder each time Hank gave his standard reply.

And so there was no one in his bed to attend to his aching legs now. He dragged himself off the bed and hobbled to the bathroom, again, to try to relieve himself. Lately it was taking him longer and longer to piss, with less and less to show for it. Sometimes he didn't make it to the bathroom in time and the urine dribbled down his legs and onto the floor. Other times he sat like a woman on the toilet and waited, and waited for the stream to begin.

That night he vowed to see a doctor as soon as he could. The pain in his legs was relentless. He looked in the bathroom mirror and in the harsh light he saw his gray skin, sagging badly below his chin and below the dark sockets of his eyes. The stubble of beard made him appear even older than he was; Hank never left the house without a close shave. But beard or no beard he hated what he saw in the mirror: an old man, the pain in his body etching lines on his face. He began to sweat, and wondered if it was hot in the room or if he was coming down with something. His legs buckled beneath him and he grabbed for the bathroom counter. His vision narrowed until he saw only a pinpoint of light. He fell to the floor, unconscious.

Chapter 14

Come morning, Dan Weatherford first knocked on Sprite Soledad's trailer door. He had expected to see one of Tomas' cars parked outside the trailer. When Dan saw no car, he decided to look in on Sprite. Through the trailer window he could see Sprite stirring from a reclining chair and coming toward the door. She was fully dressed, but he saw her smooth her hair as she neared the door.

"Mornin' Sprite," he called out.

"Dan --what are you doing here? Is everything all right?" Sprite asked anxiously. She wasn't used to seeing a deputy sheriff at her door and she immediately worried that there was bad news.

"Oh, yeah, don't worry, everything is okay as far as I know. I was going to ask you the same thing. I thought that Tomas would be home by now. When I didn't see a car I thought I would just drop by. You know he wanted me to check on you, because of the baby, and all."

Then Dan saw that Sprite had the red-rimmed, drained face of a woman who had cried recently, and for a long time.

She saw him looking at her face and immediately put both hands on her cheeks. Her face felt swollen and warm, and her eyes felt like the wind had blown fine sand beneath the lashes.

"He hasn't come home yet, Dan," Sprite said.

Dan had seen enough domestic situations to know that something was up. "Has something happened?" he asked.

Sprite shrugged. "I don't know, Dan. I'm sure he is okay. Just delayed, I guess."

"Has he called you lately?"

"I think that he tried, last night. But I was not feeling well, and I just let it go to the answering machine. I'll listen to it later."

"Okay, Sprite. Just call me if you need to."

Dan had turned and was about to step down the metal stairs when Sprite remembered the file he had left with her. "Oh, Dan, I almost forgot," she said. "That Kingman Brick Company file. I read it over and over again last night. What a weird collection of notes."

Dan had taken off his hat and twirled it slowly between his hands. "I read it too. I don't know why Hank would keep a bunch of thank you notes all these years. I was hoping you would see something that I didn't, otherwise I'm just taking it back to Hank and asking him about it."

"Well, there is something there, I'm sure. But what it is, I don't know. The notes back and forth are unnatural. Too much the same exact wording, over too many years. People don't act like that, and they don't write like that, especially men."

"I'll just take it over to Hank's now, if you'll give it to me."

"Sure, just let me get it." From the back room Dan could hear a telephone ringing and ringing, then going into the answering machine mode. Sprite made no move to answer the phone. She retrieved the Kingman file and handed it to Dan. "If you find out anything from the sheriff, let me know will you? My curiosity is up."

* * *

Dan's curiosity was up too and he decided to find Hank right away. He drove at the speed limit to the Sheriff's Department. While he was walking toward the office he saw Bonnie headed toward the Coroner's office. "Bonnie," he called out, "Hold on."

She waited for Dan. They walked together into the shared entry to the back hallways between the Sheriff's Department and the Coroner's Department. She would be going to work at his office after lunch. She always looked forward to working with Dan.

"I don't see Hank's car out in the lot," Dan said.

"I haven't seen him either, but I'm just punching in."

"How is the project going? Are you locating any more death certificates?" Dan asked.

"Quite a few. I think there are a lot more, but with a different cause of death. Especially those that say pneumonia. I'm learning quite a bit about cancer. It's interesting."

"How is your Dad doing?"

"We're holding a sand painting sing for him. Didn't I tell you?

Dan smacked his forehead. "Of sure you did. I'm sorry that I forgot. When is it, again?"

Bonnie put her left arm on his chest. She looked up at him. "It starts today."

"I'm so sorry."

There were tears in Bonnie's eyes.

"I'm putting everything that I own in this, Dan. I even took out a loan to raise money to hold the full nine days. Mom has been cooking and cooking. Thank God the corn crop is strong this year."

"I need to check in with Hank about the Kingman Brick Company situation."

"I mentioned it to my dad. He said he used to work there. A lot of other men from the Reservation worked there too, back in the sixties and seventies. He said a lot of those men have died. I told him we're looking into that."

"Let's talk about that more. I wonder where Hank could be?"

"I'll see you after lunch."

"Okay, great."

Dan stopped at the coffee pot and poured a cup. Hank's office was dark. When was the last time that happened? Hank practically lived in the office and he was an early riser.

Dan asked the secretary to call Hank, and to put him through to his office phone when she had him on the line.

Five minutes later, the secretary reported that she couldn't reach Hank on any number.

Dan sighed. "Well, I need to talk with him. Guess I'll cruise out to his house and see if his car is there."

"If he comes in while you're gone, I'll call you on your cell phone."

"Thanks," Dan said, "See you later."

* * *

The dark brown sedan was parked in the driveway at Sheriff Andrews's ranch style home. Dan pulled up near the mailbox on the side of the street and looked at the car and house. There was no noise, and no sign of life. Dan walked quickly to the door and rang the bell.

The sound echoed through the house with no response. He rang again, and listened. No response of footsteps, lights being turned on, nothing. Dan walked to the picture window and leaned toward the gap in the curtains inside. He cupped his face with both hands to afford a better view inside. He tapped on the window. Nothing.

Back at the doorbell, Dan became more and more uneasy. He began to rap on the wood door. No sign of life.

Dan called Hank's home phone from his cell phone. He could hear the telephone inside the home ringing, and ringing. No answer. Reluctantly, he tried the door. To his surprise, it wasn't locked.

He opened the door. "Hank? You there?" he called out.

Dan hated going in but felt that he had to. He walked to the center of the living room and noticed a hallway light shining. Following the light, and calling out, he saw that a hallway door was open and another light on inside. He stepped toward the light and saw bare feet protruding into the doorway. Looking in, he had a full view of Hank Andrews sprawled in soiled underwear on the bathroom floor.

Chapter 15

Sprite was already up from Dan Weatherford's unexpected visit to the trailer. She brushed her teeth and brushed her long hair, but didn't bother to change the clothes that she had just slept in. She wanted to get out of the trailer as quickly as possible. Ignoring the flashing message light on her answering machine, she picked up a light jacket and headed for her truck. She would stop at the Coop for a cup of coffee and choke down an egg sandwich for the baby's sake. Sprite had no appetite at all.

The Coop was full of coffee smells and steam from the grill. Nick was glad to see her but his dark eyes noticed right away that something was not right. Sprite looked pale and sad. The skin around her eyes was puffy. She had been crying.

Quickly he guided her to a booth and sat her down. "Don't move," he said. "I'll make sure you get a cup of coffee right away."

Sprite saw him motion to Possum, who was bringing a rack of porcelain coffee cups out of the back kitchen, to get a cup to her. Sprite was grateful for the attention.

Suddenly she longed for her former life when her morning started with a brisk walk or bike ride along the asphalt road from the trailer park to her tiny law office in the back addition off the restaurant. When she dawdled most mornings over the newspaper and several cups of coffee, and when she could wear her size 5 jeans. It seemed a lifetime ago.

Tears began to form behind her sore eyelids and she sat with her palms pressed against her face, feeling fat and lonely and very, very angry, all at once. Possum appeared with a cup and a full pot of coffee.

"Hi, Sprite," he said. "Why are you crying?"

Possum loved Sprite; she was one of the people who were always kind to him, even when he was sick like last year, before he began taking the medicine he needed. Nick was good to him too. He had a place to go now and made a small hourly wage helping Nick at the restaurant. And he got to watch Gigi, the new waitress. But today was not starting off right. He had spilled coffee behind the counter. And now Sprite was looking sad and mad at the same time.

"I'm not crying," Sprite said, wiping away tears.

"What's wrong?" Possum persisted.

"I don't want to talk about it, Possum. I just want to be left alone."

"Okay, I'm sorry, ma'am..." he began. Sprite cut him off. "Possum, look, I don't mean to take it out on you. I'm just having a bad day. I'll...I'll come back later. Just put my coffee in a cup to go."

Possum felt a little better. "I'm going to put a doughnut in a bag for you to eat later. That always makes me feel better, eating doughnuts."

Sprite gave him a weak smile. It was good to be treated kindly; she needed that more than she knew. She looked down at her growing lap and Possum looked too. "It looks like I've been eating too many doughnuts."

Possum blushed. He knew that she was having a baby soon, but all that stuff was kind of embarrassing to him. He had even seen women lift up their shirts in public and give milk to their babies. He didn't want to stare but couldn't help himself. He wondered if Sprite would be lifting up her shirt after the baby was born. He turned away to go put her coffee and doughnut in a bag. He was just glad that she had stopped crying. And he wondered where Tomas was. He was usually here with her in the morning for coffee.

Sprite squeezed beneath the steering wheel of her truck and headed north on the road to Desert View. She would have time to stop briefly to see Clara and Bonnie and Jim, but needed the mindlessness of the open road to calm down. Whatever Tomas was up to, she would be fine. She was strong and independent and used to being on her own. She could even handle raising a child by herself, if she had to. She could handle the illness on her own if she had to.

She hoped that she would not have to.

* * *

Clara was cleaning house and baking bread and corn pudding in a frenzy. Jim had been too weak to go to work that day and had stayed in his underwear in his bed. He knew that the healer would be there around suppertime, but he would not eat. Fasting was an important part of the ritual. The healer had to be a pure, empty vessel to access his full healing powers.

The smell of spicy meat filled the home. Clara wanted Jim to eat some; he had always enjoyed her cooking. It upset her when she took him some meat in a small bowl and he closed his eyes and turned his body toward the wall. He had not even tried to eat today.

Clara's own healing cures involved teas made from herbs gathered in the scrub forests that ringed the canyons near their home. She had walked many miles in the week before the healing in order to find and cut special herbs. She had gathered plenty of sage and dried it in baskets set out in the hot sunlight. The family and the healer would make sage bundles and set them on fire, then extinguish the flame and smudge the home and the hogan with the smoke from the sage bundle. Purification of the home and hogan was as important as the purification of the healer's body through fasting.

Bonnie would be home from work just about the same time as Hosteen Clah III was scheduled to arrive. She might even be home a little early on this special day. Bonnie's child, Clay, was already with her grandparents in the family home. He played with a stack of pots and pans and a wooden spoon on the kitchen floor. The banging of the spoon on the metal was getting on Clara's nerves but it kept the child happy. If it bothered Jim, he showed no sign, but simply lay with his eyes closed in his bed.

Clara hoped that Jim would at least get up and put on some clothes, shave and comb his hair before the healer arrived. She was ashamed of the way he looked today and wanted him to make an effort for the esteemed healer. Off and on during the day Clara poked her head into the bedroom and said "Come on, Jim, get up. Hosteen Clah III will be here--you've got to wash up, and put on clean clothes."

Jim wanted to get up and get dressed but it seemed like so much work. He was so tired today that he didn't want to move from the bed. He had a bad headache and his legs felt too weak to hold him up if he were to try to walk. If he rested perhaps he would gain the strength a little later to wash and dress. He felt his chin; there was stubble there that needed to be scraped away. If only he could lift his arms...

Jim fell asleep and when he awoke he heard Bonnie's voice in the kitchen, talking with Clara and then another voice, one that he didn't recognize. Apparently the healer had arrived and they were all making the last minute arrangements for the extended ceremony. Hosteen Clah III required the full payment in advance, nonrefundable. Jim was touched that Bonnie had worked hard and saved the money, but he wondered if it would all be for nothing. He knew that Dr. Lieber had a dim view of the native healing ceremonies. When Jim had talked to him about a healing that he had attended, Dr. Lieber had grunted and frowned.

Jim made himself get up. He wrapped himself in a blanket and hurried across the hallway into the bathroom. He would not dishonor his family by appearing before the healer without bathing and shaving. When he eventually appeared in the steamy kitchen, he had put on his best jeans and his one white shirt, with a string tie. His wet hair was parted on the side and slicked down. He wiped his boots with a washcloth until the leather shone in the bathroom light.

Clara hugged him when she saw him, clearly relieved that he had cleaned up for the healer. She offered him a sandwich and a cup of her tea, and he took both. His appetite had come back with the fragrance of the bread baking in the oven and the pots of cooked meat and corn on the stove. Every container in the house was filled, and Bonnie was getting ready to take some of the dishes to the neighbor's house and ask them to store it for the coming crowd. Jim was getting excited about seeing everyone and hearing them chant and dance for his healing.

Clara was flushed with the heat and excitement of hosting the great healer. Her own healing ideas were in her mind, but she said nothing. It would have been presumptuous to share her thoughts with such a revered healer. She wanted to ask him a dozen questions, but he seemed unapproachable; almost in an altered state of mind already. She decided to wait, and watch, and learn. When Jim had finished his second cup of tea the healer took him by the arm. Together they left the kitchen to head to the ceremonial hogan.

Chapter 16

Sprite had taken her time driving to Desert View. She had her cell phone with her, but it was silent. She wished that she had listened to the messages that she knew were on her home answering machine, but she was not ready to hear Tomas' voice.

Sprite found Ed hard at work, helping the drywall crew slap mud onto the cracks in the drywall. After the first coat was dried it would be sanded down and then mudded again, then sanded smooth before the primer was rolled on to the drywall. It was hard and tedious work, but the crew moved with practiced motions of arms and hands and was making good progress. When Ed saw Sprite he motioned for her to go outside. He didn't want her breathing the dust that hung in the air like a mist.

Once outside Ed pulled off his safety glasses. The outline of the goggles remained on his face. Sweat streamed down his temples and left tiny gullies in the crust of drywall dust. It was still morning but the temperatures had already reached 85 degrees. It had been a sunny but hot October. Sprite was hoping for continued good weather so that the work on the house could continue. Ed had been working six days a week. On Sundays he insisted on resting and visiting his family in Flagstaff. Sprite approved of Ed, both for his hard work habits, his insistence on the highest quality construction for the home, and his dedication to his family. Tomas could learn a few things from Ed, she thought.

From the outside deck they entered the family room so that Sprite could see the results of the windows that he had finished installing since the last time that she was there. Together they climbed the stairway to the large room that would be the heart of the home. Sprite was struck by its spare beauty. The wood floors had not yet been finished but she could imagine how they would glow. The walls when painted would be painted white, the better to reflect the color of the sky at sunrise or sunset. And the panoramic, floor to ceiling expanse of glass afforded a dramatic view of the steep ravine. Sprite stood at the window and took it in. But her mind was still churning with hurt over Tomas' behavior. Why would he throw all of this away?

Ed noticed her silent brooding. He came and stood beside and noticed, but didn't speak of, her red-rimmed eyes that were shining with uncried tears and anger. To distract her and to break the long silence, he said "Look over there, at that ridge of rock about two-thirds of the way from the bottom of the ravine. Do you see the drawing?"

Sprite squinted at the sunlight overhang and remembered when she was here before. She had seen a crude but definite outline of something—it looked like a bird then, maybe a hawk. She looked at Ed. "Yes, I see it, but I can't tell what it is."

"I'm not sure, but if I had to guess I would say an eagle."

"That would be better than what I see. I thought it was a hawk."

Ed peered through the glass again. "I can't be sure," he admitted.

"I'm going to go outside and look around a little. It is such a beautiful day. And I've got a lot on my mind."

"I'll just finish up with the wall we're working on downstairs. When you are done walking, let me know. I have a thermos of coffee in the trailer that I can share."

"That would be so nice," Sprite said.

The air was brisk near the ravine. It refreshed Sprite, and she was less aware of the scent of her clothing that she had slept in. The scratchiness behind her tired eyes was soothed by the slight breeze. The sky was a perfect blue. Sprite walked the length of the ravine on their property, then remembered that she wanted to try to get a closer look at the bird drawing or carving. It was exciting to think that it might be an ancient petroglyph, one of the thousands of etchings made by a lost culture in the caverns, and on canyon walls, across Arizona, New Mexico, Utah and Colorado. She had seen them before in the state and federal parks but never dreamed that she would see one from her own window.

Suddenly, Sprite felt lighter. Her spirits lifted and she forgot for the moment her disappointment and anger at Tomas. The lightly wooded ravine was like a scene from a dream that she had dreamed for years. When she wanted peace of mind, this was the landscape she sought. In her reverie Sprite began a slow dance, and despite her belly she managed to step gracefully and to turn in large circles. She opened her arms wide and held them high, spreading her fingers wide and pulling at the air as if trying to catch a white cloud as it moved across the sky. She closed her eyes and tilted her face to feel the warm rays of sunlight bathe her brown skin, and dry any tears that had escaped her thick lashes.

Sprite felt the weight of the child but it did not hold her down just then but rather rocked gently inside her in its own little sea. She began to think of how it looked, sweetly smiling, perhaps, at the feeling of being lifted up, then around, then down. She had just begun to sing out loud when her toe caught an exposed cypress root and her momentum sent her, off-balance now, into a washed out section of the ravine lip. She tried to grab a branch of the cypress but it was dried and brittle and broke off rather than catching her fall. Sprite yelled sharply and from inside the lowest level of the home Ed and the drywallers looked up to see a flash of colored cloth and brown boot as Sprite disappeared into the ravine.

Chapter 17

Tomas was starting to get anxious. He had been calling Spirit on her home phone with no answer. He was unable to get through to her cell phone; his own cell phone registered "no service" when he called. Now Dan Weatherford was unavailable; he had left two messages already for Dan with no return call.

His irritation with Casey grew with his inability to reach Spirit. The interstate highway had finally reopened--at least for a period of time. More rain was predicted. The Aston Martin was a great car, but a poor boat, and that's what Tomas felt he was commanding as he reached the spot where they had left Casey's Jeep the day before. There was still standing water around the Jeep. Tomas waded into it and replaced the battery. When he fired the ignition, the Jeep stirred to life and after one false hiccup when the engine died (probably from water in the systems), it ran smoothly enough for Casey to drive it. He followed her for a short distance to be sure that she was on her way before he passed her, giving her a brief wave of his hand before kicking up the Vanquish to an acceptable, to him if not the law, cruising speed.

Finally, he muttered. I'm at least a day behind schedule. The girl needed my help but damn, don't they all.

Tomas wondered how long he would be cut off from cell phone service from Spirit. Just then his own cell phone rang. It was Dan Weatherford.

Tomas leapt on him. "What's going on out there?" he hollered. The road noise was deafening as he passed semi after semi which slapped water from their eighteen wheels onto his silver Vanquish. It would take him an entire day to clean it when he got to Arizona.

"You won't believe it."

"Try me," Tomas said sullenly.

"Hank Andrews had a heart attack sometime last night."

"Jesus," said Tomas. "Is he alive?"

"Yes, but he is going to have open heart surgery today. He has several arteries close to being completely shut off. They will do a quadruple bypass, and there is still no guarantee that he will survive the operation. He'll be out of commission for a long time."

"Who found him?" Tomas thought that whoever it was, Hank owed him his life.

"I did. I went over to his house when he didn't show up at work. You know he hasn't missed a day's work, ever, as far as I can remember. His car was in the driveway but no one came to the door. It was unlocked. I went in and found him on the bathroom floor. The ambulance was there in another fifteen minutes and the guys took over."

"Unbelievable."

Dan remembered that he wanted to talk to Tomas about Sprite. He wasn't sure how to broach the subject so he just waded in. "Tomas, I saw Sprite this morning before I found Hank. She didn't look too well."

Tomas felt panic rising like flood waters in his chest. "What do you mean?"

"Well, uh, she looked like she hadn't slept at all. Her eyes were swollen like she had been crying."

"What did she say?"

"Not much, and I didn't want to butt in or anything. I figured you two had a fight on the telephone. She looked the way my wife looks after we have had a big argument."

Dan knew well how a woman looks when she is angry and hurt. Truth was, he saw too much of that at home. Sometimes his wife accused him of having an affair, he was gone away from home so often.

"I haven't spoken to Spirit for a couple of days. I ran into closed roads in Arkansas due to flooding. Had to stay overnight."

"Oh, sorry, I didn't know. Well, maybe she was just worried about you."

"She didn't know anything about it. I tried to call but no one picked up at the trailer, and I can't get service through to her cell."

"When do you expect to be back?"

"Not until early tomorrow morning. Do you mind checking on her again tonight, Dan? I'd really appreciate it."

"Sure, I'll be going to the hospital to see how Hank is doing, then I'll swing by Sprite's office. Did you try calling her there?"

"I did but only got the answering machine there too."

"Well if she is not there I'll go back to the trailer. Don't worry, I'll find her and then I'll ask her to call you or I'll call myself. It'll be okay, I'm sure."

They hung up.

Tomas was not totally reassured. Why would Spirit have been awake all night?

* * *

Dan thought about the evening ahead and remembered that tonight was the sing for Jim Hammer. That made three or four places he needed to go before he went home: the hospital, Sprite's office and home, and Jim's house. He remembered they lived somewhere out near the Reservation but he wasn't exactly sure where.

Thinking about Jim reminded Dan that he had better get back to his own office. Bonnie was holding down the phones while Dan kept up on the status of Hank Andrews' surgery, but she wanted to go home early because of the sing. He could certainly understand that; a sing would be as well attended as a wedding feast and would last a lot longer. The family was put to work and kept cooking and feeding the gathering until the last dancer left the hogan. No wonder people were opting for the two day, or the five day, instead of the entire nine days. Most people could scarce afford to feed their own families, much less the entire community.

Bonnie and Dan had talked of little but the coming sing, but they were able to devote an hour to the Kingman Brick Company assignment. Dan told Bonnie what Sprite had said about the file: that it was completely unnatural. Bonnie had not seen the file so Dan showed her the letters and cards sent over the years between Cal Kingman and Hank. Bonnie agreed that there was something wrong about the exchanges, but she had no idea what it could mean.

"Why don't you just ask Hank?" she said.

"Come on, Bonnie, I can't do that now. I was planning to, before I found him this morning. If he lives, I will ask him eventually. I'm just not sure why he gave me this file."

Bonnie was embarrassed. She had momentarily forgotten about Hank's condition. She was far too preoccupied with her own father to think straight. "Oh, Dan, I'm an idiot," she said.

"No, it's okay. I forget myself. He is always just here. I didn't even know he was sick. What do you think I should do with his gun? It was on his kitchen table this morning. I didn't feel right leaving it out like that. You know, anybody could see it through the window and just break in."

"You did the right thing, Dan."

"Maybe we should lock it in his desk."

Bonnie said, "That's a good idea. Why don't I do it, you've had a long day."

"Okay, thanks. Right now it is in his office, in his belt, hanging on the coat rack."

"Don't worry, I'll take care of it."

Dan gunned the cruiser and headed for the hospital. Once there he was told that the Sheriff was still in surgery but that everything seemed to be progressing as well as could be expected. There was no point in staying there: no family waited in the waiting room. The desk nurse at the surgical center took Dan's card and agreed that he would be allowed to call later to check on Hank's condition.

Dan remembered to call his wife before he headed out to

Sprite's office. As shocked as she was to hear about the Sheriff, she didn't understand why Dan had to work late. "Why do you feel like you have to take care of the whole world? You're there to help everybody except your own family. I stay at home with the kids and the dishes and the dirty laundry while you drive around making sure everyone else is feeling good…"

Dan could hear the sullen anger in her voice. It was getting to be her normal tone of voice. And it made him want to stay away from home even later. Maybe she would be asleep by the time he came in.

He put his wife's mood out of his mind. Pointing the squad car in the direction of Sprite's office, he gunned the engine and turned on the radio for company.

The windows of the Coop were lit and steamy from the late diners, but there was no sign of anyone in Sprite's law office out back. Dan decided to have a cup of coffee before checking at her trailer.

Possum was wiping the counter with a suspiciously grimy towel when Dan swung his long legs under the ledge and motioned toward the coffee pot. Possum looked toward the pot. "Isn't it kind of late for coffee?" Possum asked

"Never too late for a policeman to be drinking coffee," joked Dan. "We live on the stuff. It's like how cars use gasoline."

Possum poured his coffee. "Have you seen Sprite Soledad in here today?"

Possum looked down. He wasn't sure what the answer should be. When police asked him questions, he was usually in trouble, at least before he started working here at the Coop. Dan noticed his discomfort. "It's okay, Possum. I'm just trying to make sure she's okay."

Possum remembered Sprite's tears from the morning. "Well she was here, for breakfast. She ordered and then said no, never mind. She was in a hurry I guess."

"Did she say where she was going?"

"No."

"Did she seem okay, you know, normal acting?"

Possum thought it over, and decided he could trust Dan. He knew that Dan Weatherford and Sprite were friends. "She was crying a little."

"Well, I guess I'll go over to her house and see if she is okay."

Nick Costa came around the corner from the kitchen to greet Dan. At this time, there were no other customers in the restaurant and he could spare a moment. He poured himself a cup of coffee along the way, then sank down on a stool by Dan.

Possum looked at Nick and said, "Did you need some gasoline too?"

Nick looked confused, and decided to ignore the kid. Possum often said unusual things and Nick routinely ignored him. He figured it went with the territory of Possum's mental condition. At least he was making sense most of the time, ever since he started taking his medicine. Sprite had seen to it that Possum went to a doctor and obtained a prescription to help him think more clearly and be able to express himself in a logical way. Most of the time.

Dan told Nick he was looking for Sprite, that Tomas was delayed in coming back from Atlanta and had not been able to reach Sprite.

"Haven't seen her since early morning," Nick said. "Usually she'll come in for lunch, but not today. She looked pretty rough this morning, but you know how it is with pregnant women. Good days and bad days when they are as far along as Sprite."

Nick didn't need to tell Dan about pregnant women and their moods. The thought struck him that his wife might be pregnant, again. His stomach clenched at the thought, and then he felt guilty about not wanting any more kids. He would have to be more careful, he guessed.

Dan drained his cup and stood up stiffly. Then he remembered Hank and snapped his fingers. "Nick, I nearly forgot to tell you. The sheriff had a heart attack or something last night. I went out to his place when he didn't show up at the office. He was there, kind of semiconscious and not able to talk too well. I thought maybe it was a stroke. Called the ambulance; they took him to the hospital. He's still in surgery there."

Nick pulled out a cigarette and lit it. He took in the information seriously, and would dole it out to the regular customers in his usual way. That's the way things were done in Hidden City. People got the news from one another, or they waited for the weekly newspaper to come out. With this kind of news chances were good that everyone in town would know Hank's condition long before the article hit the paper.

"That's real tough, Dan. I guess you are going to have to take charge, huh?"

"At least for a while," Dan admitted. "But he's a tough guy. I think he'll pull through, or he wouldn't have made it this far."

Nick tapped his ash off the cigarette with a practiced index finger. "Speaking of tough guys, isn't this the first night of the sing for Bonnie Hammer's dad?"

Dan nodded his head. "Everything seems to be happening all at once. I'm hoping to get out there for a little while. Bonnie asked me to come. But first I need to make sure that Sprite is okay and then let Tomas know."

"Why don't you just call Sprite?"

Dan saw the sense in that. He was just so accustomed to patrolling in his car that he forgot the phone. He asked Possum to bring him the telephone book. Her home telephone number was listed. Dan called. The phone rang five times and then went into the answering machine. He left a message. Now he was even more worried. He would have to drive there to make sure that she was not well enough to pick up the phone. With a sigh, he slapped Nick lightly on the shoulder and said "Guess I'd better go check." Nick nodded and stubbed out his cigarette.

* * *

Sprite's trailer was as dark as her office had been. When Dan knocked on the trailer door, hard, he could hear Bunny, Sprite's bulldog, whimpering and clawing at the door. Peering through the plexiglass, it appeared that everything was exactly the same as when he was there this morning. The dog was barking then and Dan wondered if the animal had been shut inside all day.

Dan called Tomas' cell phone number from his own cell phone. He didn't want to alarm Tomas, but something here was not right.

Tomas answered on the first ring. Dan could hear the road noise, and guessed that Tomas was going as fast as he could. "I'm going to put you on the speaker phone," Tomas said.

Dan told Tomas slowly and clearly that he was at the trailer, but that Sprite was not there. The dog was barking constantly now, and jumping at the door. It was hard to hear above the frantic animal's din.

Tomas heard the commotion in the background. "Jesus," he said, "what's going on with the dog?"

"My guess is she hasn't been out all day."

"Dan, there is a spare key to the trailer taped up under the bottom shelf in the storage shed. Please get it and let yourself in."

"Okay. I don't think Sprite is in there though. Her truck isn't here."

"Do you mind letting the dog out?"

"No, I'll do that. I'll call you back, all right? I need both hands here."

"Okay. Let me know if anything seems out of place in the trailer."

"Sure."

Except for the pent-up dog, Dan didn't see anything unusual in the trailer. Certainly there was no evidence of a struggle, or a break-in. No, Sprite had gone somewhere, that's all. It wasn't like her to neglect her dog, but Dan figured that she had probably just gotten tied up with a client, that's all.

Chapter 18

Clara watched her husband enter the ceremonial hogan through the east door. Hosteen Clah III seated himself as required at the west wall facing the door on a woven rug. He beat on the taut skin of a drum, slowly, rhythmically, and began:

From the beginning there were drums, the booming, never failing four seasons, gliding smoothly one to the other; when the birds come and when they go, the bear taking his winter sleep and waking in the spring. Watch the heartbeat in your wrist—a steady beat of life's drum...

Jim lay down on another brightly colored woven rug near the medicine man.

The healer began to peer through the open doorway into the East. The east was the beginning of all things, fresh starts each day with the arrival of the dawn. The east would bring a new beginning for Jim, a healing of his body and his spirit. Of that Hosteen Clah III had no doubt. He was confident, he was strong and after his days of fasting and prayer he felt close to the divine and in harmony with the healing forces. He remembered his connection with the sacred that had come from his great-grandfather. Hosteen was the holiest of holy men, fortunate to have been born both male and female He had all the blessings of Father Sky and Mother Earth. He was truly in balance and was able to help many others to regain their natural balance and to return to health to walk in harmony once again. Hosteen Clah III fell silent while he thanked his great-grandfather for passing along his power to him and asked that he might be present within him during the long days to come.

Clara sat on the west half of the hogan door as tradition for women demanded. She took out a small notebook and pencil in order to make notes for herself. As worried as she was about her husband, she was secretly thrilled to have a vantage point to view the entire healing ceremony. She couldn't write as quickly as the shaman was speaking, but each of his prayers would be repeated tonight and during the nights to come, so that by the end of the healing she would have a complete version of the ceremony.

The Blessing Way chant was powerful and sacred. Clara knew that it was not to be written down perfectly—only the gods were perfect—and flaws in humans were taken for granted. It was also important to protect the sanctity of the Navajo people's ritual from the curious eyes and ears of the white people. And so her notes were deliberately flawed, just as the woven rugs and the sand paintings—at least one intentional "mistake" lest the gods be offended that humans strove for their perfection.

The shaman intoned:

...in the house made of dawn,
...in the house made of evening twilight,
...in the house made of dark cloud,
...in the house made of male rain,
...in the house made of dark mist,
...in the house made of female rain,
...in the house made of pollen,
...in the house made of grasshoppers,
Where the dark mist curtains the doorway,
The path to which is on the rainbow,
Where the zig-zag lightning stands on top,
Where the he-man rain stands high on top,
Oh, male divinity!
With your moccasins of dark cloud, come to us
With your leggings of dark cloud, come to us.
With your shirt of dark cloud, come to us.
With your headdress of dark cloud, come to us...

* * *

A sheriff's squad car was pulling into the driveway beyond Clara's house. She slipped the notebook into her apron pocket and stood up. She felt the stiffness of her back from the time spent sitting on the ground in the hogan. She scratched at an insect bite on her right shin. Dan Weatherford stepped out of the car. He removed his hat and left it in the car. Reaching into the back seat he pulled out a large brown paper bag that appeared to be heavy with groceries. Clara offered a silent prayer. Dan may not have been dressed in dark clouds, but he looked good to her as he saw her walking toward him. His shy smile warmed her as he tipped his head toward the house: "shall I put these groceries inside?"

She nodded. Dan could see wafts of smoke coming from the hogan and smelled the burning sage. He was worried that he had interrupted something private--it was not yet time for the public to gather and sing in support of the healing--but Clara's grateful smile as she met him near the kitchen door and took the bag out of his hands reduced his fear that he was committing any serious breach of behavior.

Clara spoke first. "Dan, it is good to see you."

"Clara…"

"I'm so worried about Jim. He seems so weak, so tired, today."

"It has been a bad day all over, I guess. Is Bonnie here?"

"She was just finishing up the dishes and getting ready to put Clay to bed, a little while ago." Clara stepped into the kitchen and called out "Bonnie?"

From the back room he heard a noise. Then Bonnie's flushed face appeared from around the hallway corner. "Dan! I'm surprised to see you, after all that happened today."

Clara looked puzzled.

"Mom, Sheriff Andrews had a bad heart attack or something today. Dan found him in his bathroom at home, and the ambulance took him to the hospital," Bonnie explained. She looked up at Dan. "How is he doing?"

"Okay, I guess. I'll need to check back in with the nurse in a little while."

"Please, Dan, sit down. Would you like some coffee?"

"Just a little," said Dan. "I had some back at the Coop." He hesitated and then decided to ask the next question. "Say, did either of you happen to see Sprite today? I've been looking for her. I told Tomas that I would check in on her until he comes back from Atlanta, but she is not at the office or at her trailer."

Clara shook her head. "She stopped by here early today. She said that she was going up to Desert View, to check on the house that they are building up there."

"Did she seem okay?"

Clara's eyes narrowed. "Not exactly. She looked pale. But sometimes that happens you know, with pregnant women. It's not easy." Clara knew too about Sprite's illness, but out of modesty she didn't say anything about that to Dan. Dan was visibly relieved. "Did she say if she would be back here later, for the singing?"

"Well she didn't exactly say when she would come back, whether it would be tonight or tomorrow night. She didn't stay long, just enough to talk with Jim a little. And he barely got out of bed today. She seemed in kind of a hurry to get up to the house. She said the carpenter would be there."

Dan relaxed for the first time in hours. Sprite was just delayed, he was sure.

* * *

In Desert View, Ed's heart paused a beat when he glimpsed Sprite's fall into the deep ravine. Dropping his sanding block with which he had been finishing a section of the drywall on the lowest level, he called to the two young men who formed the dry walling team to follow him, there had been an accident. With one hand he flipped open his cell phone and punched in 911. He took the stairs two at a time and was rounding the corner of the home headed toward the last spot he had seen Sprite, when the call went through to Emergency services. "I'm working at a new house just southeast of Desert View," he said. "The owner's wife fell-tripped, I think- and fell into the ravine. I can't see her yet."

"What's your name, sir?"

"Ed. I'm building the house. Oh, wait, maybe you should

know that she is pregnant. Pretty far along too, maybe eight months? I'm not exactly sure."

"We're on the way. Tell me exactly where the house is located."

Ed was at the spot where he saw Sprite fall, and he looked over the edge, hoping...

"The nearest cross road coming from Desert View is Vinegar Creek Road. It's about five miles from Desert View. The house is on the left side; that would be on the east side of the highway. It's tall-two and a half stories above ground. There will be work trucks in the driveway."

The dispatcher was calm but said "Try to get any cars and trucks out of the way before we pull in. If there is anyone there who can stand out by the road and direct us in, get someone out there."

"Okay, yes, I can do that." "JORGE! I've got the ambulance people on the phone. Get out by the road, would you? And move those trucks out of the way. We need to clear a path. Stay by the road to direct them in, and hurry."

Jorge looked disappointed to be sent away from the edge but did as he was told.

Ed looked down and saw Sprite, slumped against a cypress about ten feet down. She was moving her head and saying something, he couldn't hear what. One arm seemed to be at on odd angle.

The dispatcher said, "Tell me what you see."

"I can see her now. She's moving a little," he said.

"Can you get to her without falling yourself?"

"I-I don't know. Maybe with a rope to tie off—Carlos—go get a rope, por favor. I'm going down to see."

Carlos jogged off to the house, hoping to find a rope. Maybe they could use a ladder.

"Tell her not to move," the dispatcher said.

"SPRITE," Ed yelled, "Don't try to move. I'm coming down. Just stay still."

She didn't turn to look at him, but he thought he heard her

moan. He didn't see any blood. Carlos came with the rope. He tied one end of the rope to a small tree at the top of the ravine. Ed placed the cell phone into his shirt breast pocket and rappelled down the side of the ravine. He was glad it was only about ten feet. He was afraid of heights. When he reached Sprite he spoke again with the 911 dispatcher.

Sprite looked at him with dull eyes. "Ed?" she asked. What happened to me?

"You tripped, I think. There is a root up above that had pushed out of the ground."

The dispatcher broke in, "Is she alert?"

Time slowed to a crawl until the emergency vehicles pulled in to the rough driveway. Jorge motioned the EMTs to go to the back of the lot. Ed heard the jangle of metal as they set up the gurney and then he saw faces up above. One of the EMTs began to rappel on the rope Carlos had set up.

"Good job," said the EMT. "We can take it from here." He went to Sprite and saw that she was conscious. He shined a penlight into her eyes, one after the other. The medic listened to her heartbeat with a stethoscope and took her blood pressure. He called the number up to his team and then began to examine Sprite, tenderly touching her legs and arms and asking her questions. "Can you feel this? Can you feel this?"

She seemed to be intact, except for her left arm. It hung crookedly from high up, near the shoulder. There was no bone protruding. There was no way of knowing the damage without taking X-rays and CT scans. The second EMT had lowered a sling. Carefully the medic transferred Sprite into the sling and with Ed's help from beneath, and the EMT, Jorge and Carlos pulling from above, Sprite was raised up the wall of the ravine. She was talking, but Ed could not make out what she was saying. "Whew," he said when she was stretched out on the gurney, a sheet placed over her rounded abdomen, "that was close." His hands were starting to tremble and he was not able to make them quiet.

The medic turned to him. "Are you okay, sir?"

The dispatcher was now in touch with the EMTs. "I'll be fine. As long as she is okay, I'll be okay."

"Are you her husband?"

"Oh, no, her husband is out of state, on his way back from Atlanta or somewhere. I'm building this house for them."

The EMT looked up at the modern structure. The all-glass side towered over another section of the ravine. "Great view. Nice place. Wish I could afford it."

"Yeah, thanks. Me too. And maybe someday. Right now I'm just glad that she's going to be okay. What about the baby?"

"As far as we can tell right now, her worst problem is that broken arm. Get in touch with the husband and let him know that we're taking her to the hospital at Desert View. It's a pretty small hospital and if she has any serious internal injuries she'll be transferred to somewhere else. But that's where she'll be going first. He handed Ed a card with the telephone number of the Desert View Hospital. He can call this number."

"Thank you. I'll try to call him right away."

"It's a good thing that you were here. No one would have known where to look if you had not seen her go over the side. What was she doing out there, anyway?"

"It looked like she was dancing."

The medic raised both eyebrows.

Chapter 19

When Tomas received the call from Ed, that Spirit was in the hospital with a probable broken arm, Tomas defied the speed limit in two states to get home.

But when he finally arrived at the hospital in Desert View and tried to take her in his arms, she turned away in stony silence. She refused to look at him or to say a word. When he asked the doctors about her, they shrugged and said she had suffered a broken arm; that they had set the fracture and that she appeared to be otherwise fine. She would need a short period of physical therapy after the cast was removed. Sprite would be fine, they said.

He was embarrassed to tell them that his own wife would not speak to him, or look at him. Spirit was released from the hospital after one night--for observation--and was now back at the trailer. She hugged the dog and talked softly to her pet, but ignored Tomas and turned her back to him when he attempted to kiss her.

Finally, Tomas snapped at her, "Look, Spirit, I don't know what happened while I was gone. But this is bullshit. Just tell me what I did to upset you because I sure can't read your mind."

Spirit knew that if she looked at him, she would start crying again. She was glad that her fall had resulted in only a broken arm, and that the baby was unharmed, but she was carrying inside her a broken heart that was rapidly turning into a cold stone. If she had known how to talk to Tomas, she would have. But if she tried to open her mouth to talk to him just now, she would only let out a cold gust of air. The words would freeze into barbed shards of anger and disappointment, fall to the trailer floor, and shatter.

The silent moment grew longer and when it became clear to Tomas that she was not going to answer him, he got up. Running his hand across his road-tired eyes he turned and left the trailer. She heard him get in and quickly turn the car around in the gravel driveway. With a long, sustained push on the gas pedal, he was gone.

Spirit lay on her side for a long time, trying to hear the sound of the car's engine. Tears filled her closed eyes but she refused to let them escape. She had cried enough. Now she needed to plan; to figure out just how she would make it through the baby's birth on her own. Maybe she could find a local woman to help her, someone who had children of her own and knew how to take care of a baby.

* * *

Hosteen Clah III was having trouble keeping his patient awake. Jim was fading in and out of consciousness. Increasingly, he slept. Hosteen Clah III needed a patient who participated. As dawn crept in he longed for sleep himself, in spite of the demands of the healing he was drawn to the closed eyes and soft breathing of his patient. He tried to concentrate on the chant and called louder:

...with the far darkness made of the dark cloud on the ends of your wings, come to us soaring.

...with the darkness on the earth, come to us.

I have made your sacrifice.

I have prepared a smoke for you.

Gratefully Hosteen Clah III drew his tobacco pouch from the plaited cord around his neck and pinched out the ceremonial tobacco. He placed it in his pipe, a foot long piece of deer antler, that had been carefully hollowed and a bowl for the tobacco scraped out of one antler tip. The pipe had been in the Clah family for many decades. It was worn smooth from being passed from man to man, and the striations of the antlers were almost gone; it was down to satiny bone. He puffed on the pipe and gazed at the gaunt man who lay on the blanket in the hogan, surrounded by the sand painting that Hosteen had completed in the night.

It was a good painting and yet there was something not right with the situation. He moved closer to the man and leaned forward to examine him. At this point they should be praying together, something like this:

...my limbs restore for me,
...my body restore for me.
...my mind restore for me.
...my voice restore for me...
...today take away your spell for me.
...far off from me it is taken.
And then:
...happily I recover.
...happily my limbs regain their power.
...happily my head becomes cool again.
...happily I hear again.
...happily I walk.
Impervious to pain, I walk.
Feeling light within, I walk...

Hosteen Clah III knew that it was not working. Jim's breathing had changed in the night and had become a snore and then more congested. His mouth had drawn onto a pale "O" as his lungs labored to take in oxygen. Hosteen Clah III had never lost a patient and he didn't intend to lose this one. He prayed harder, chanted louder, and drew sand paintings with the carefully prepared tints one more beautiful than the next. The sacred tobacco smoke filled the hogan.

Clara, sitting quietly just outside the hogan, had never heard such beautiful singing. The people of the community who called themselves not Navajo--that was the white man's term for them-- but Dineh--the people, the first people, filed by singing softly along with the sacred healing chants. They were gathered now in the home, drinking coffee and eating sandwiches and corn pudding. Some even forgot the solemn and sacred nature of the event and were laughing, swapping gossip and catching up on the news of the lives of the relatives and friends that had not gathered together for a while.

Clara made careful notes in her booklet and sat on her haunches, her skirts gathered about her. She was tired and twice during the night had simply stretched out on the hard soil and napped for short periods of time. She dreamed of birds, hundreds and hundreds of birds of all species. The flapping of their wings against her screen door was deafening. But one of them, a blue jay, spoke to her. It said that she would be given a gift of healing greater than all of the men, greater than Hosteen Clah III, greater than the white doctors. The people of the Reservation and beyond would revere her,

When Clara woke up her heart was pounding. She knew that a dream of birds meant that death was near. She wanted to go into the hogan to check on Jim, but she didn't dare. The shaman was deeply involved in his chanting and praying. He would not appreciate her interruption.

* * *

Tomas sat at the counter at the Coop, complaining to Nick about women. Nick had heard it all before, but listened sympathetically anyway, his large brown eyes registering Tomas' frustration. "I don't even know what I did," said Tomas.

He had gone over the events of the last few days in his mind, and couldn't fathom why Spirit would be so angry that she wouldn't even speak to him, wouldn't even look at him.

"Maybe it was because I was delayed in getting back?" Tomas wondered out loud.

"Did you call her and let her know?" Nick asked.

"I...I think so. I don't remember exactly. You see I had to help out this girl. She was stranded out on the highway with a dead battery. There were storms everywhere and standing water on the road. I took her to get a new battery. By the time we got back the state police had closed the interstate and we couldn't even get to her car to get the battery in."

Nick's radar went off. "Did you tell Sprite about that?"

"No. It wasn't important. I was just helping this girl out."

"How long did it take you to help her?

"The road was closed overnight. We stayed at a motel. In separate rooms."

Nick looked at Tomas levelly.

"And you figured she wouldn't know about it anyway, right"

"Right. Sure. How would she?"

"I don't know but my gut feeling is she knows or thinks that she knows something. I smell a jealous woman. A jealous pregnant woman."

Tomas frowned. Twin furrows appeared on his forehead, between his eyes. "I don't know, Nick."

"Better try it out. Even if she isn't talking to you, talk to her. Just mention casually what you just told me and see if she reacts. It can't get much worse if I'm wrong, can it?"

Tomas was irritated and sulking. How could she know what happened? And he was still being punished. Maybe he should have just gone for it.

Business at the diner was slow. Nick walked Tomas out to see the car. It was covered in caked on red mud from the flood in Arkansas, but Nick could see that it was one fine automobile. Tomas would spend the rest of the day washing it, cleaning the interior, and waxing. But the result would be worth it. If Spirit were talking to him again by dinnertime, he would take her for a ride. Out to dinner, maybe.

By the time Tomas returned to the trailer to draw Spirit out of her mood, she--and Bunny--were gone. Tomas sighed and searched under the kitchen sink for the cleaning bucket and rags. He was done chasing after her, broken arm or no broken arm. She was going to have to come back to him this time.

* * *

Sprite entered the gate and saw the ceremonial hogan with the smoke rising from the central vent. She felt washed out, and was drawn to the healing for herself almost as much as for Jim. But she tried to push her own needs from her mind. The power of a healing is in the community support along with the chanting and prayers and shaman's sand paintings. Her time would come, but now it was time to focus.

Clara was kneeling on a mat outside the hogan. Bonnie hovered over her, and Bonnie's child, Clay, played nearby. When the women saw Sprite they brightened. Sprite was someone in the community. They could count on her to know what to do. Today, though, Sprite was clearly different. Her arm was in a sling. Her face was puffy and the circles under her eyes denied sleep.

Bonnie walked to her and put her strong arms around her. As short as Bonnie was Sprite was shorter and yet Bonnie could feel the quiet strength coming from her round body. "What's going on?" asked Bonnie.

Sprite knew that she wasn't fooling Bonnie with her tough act. Women knew how to read a face. Suddenly the tears pooled again, and yet Sprite knew the customs. A man was in the hogan, as sick as one can be. This was serious business. The rest could wait. But it was good of Bonnie to ask. She had to be under stress as well, with her dad inside and the townspeople gathering. There were at least twenty people now, and maybe some would stay and take up the chanting and singing that night. Others would go home to waiting families. Bonnie prayed in between serving the guests.

Clara knelt again. She was weakened too, having held her vigil and maintained her composure even after the dream. She needed to be close to the earth right now. She had turned in the various directions, east, west, north, south, above and now, below. Sprite shaded her raw eyes from the glaring sun. "How is Jim?"

Clara answered: "He's trying."

Sprite took this to mean he was making the effort to live, in spite of his pain. Clara actually meant he was trying to die, but she didn't want to say anything in front of Bonnie. Bonnie was still denying the seriousness of Jim's illness, and hanging on to the healing shaman's reputation for miracles. This will work, Bonnie thought. If her own will mattered, her father would rise and walk.

Sprite nodded. "May I come in?" she asked.

Bonnie knew that she meant to the main house. "Of course, Sprite. Please be at home."

She looked again toward the hogan and saw Hosteen Clah III peering out of the east door. Sprite looked into his face and was surprised: he had broken his trance. There was no chanting, no prayer, no singing. She looked at Clara and saw that she noticed as well. Hosteen Clah III blocked the doorway and turned his back. Clara narrowed her eyes.

Then he turned around and began to pray aloud again. Soon Clara joined in, and Sprite was surprised to see that Clara knew the words. Sprite herself strove to understand but only caught part of the meaning that was something like:

...happily the young men will regard you.

...happily the young women will regard you.

...happily the chiefs will regard you.

...happily as they scatter in different directions they will regard you.

...happily as they approach their homes they will regard you.

...happily may their roads home be on the trail of pollen.

...happily may they all get back.

Clara caught Sprite's eye and nodded to her, Sprite saw the knowledge in Clara's face, and the tears in her eyes that would fall later, when her duties were done. Others might continue to have the illusion that Hosteen Clah III was healing Jim, but Clara and Sprite both knew: Jim had died. Soon they would break a hole in the north side of the hogan, to remove his body to the dark side. Bonnie mingled and tended to Clay and rose from time to time to greet new arrivals. She didn't have the keen sense of nuance or spiritual powers of her mother.

One of Clara's relatives brought Sprite a folding lawn chair. She sat down heavily near Clara. Clara had gone quiet again. Spirit thought about the ups and downs of that long marriage, but soon her thoughts turned to Tomas. She thought about her anger toward him, and then, just a glimmer of doubt as to his actions. What if she was wrong? What if there was some other explanation? He certainly had been treating her well enough. She didn't get the feeling that he would do something so low as to pick up a woman on a road trip. The more she thought it over, the more ashamed she was for not simply asking him about the odd conversation that she had with someone on his phone. If Clara could forgive Jim after the long years of drinking and fighting, maybe Sprite could work it out with Tomas. The healing atmosphere and the sight of the widow crying softly for her mate worked on Sprite's heart.

Sprite's cocky confidence of the day before, when in her hot anger she had decided that she had no need or desire for Tomas or any other man, was dissolving. As much as need she wanted to have a future with Tomas. She wanted a family, a husband, the dream home. She resolved to go to him, and confront him. If he confessed to a huge indiscretion then she would have to decide what to do.

Clara rose from her mat as Sprite told her that she would have to leave, but that she would be as close as the telephone. She made sure that Clara had her home number and told her to call if Sprite could be of help. She would be back for the public mourning and the final sing. As she walked away she spoke the final words of the Night Way:

...With beauty before me, I walk.
...With beauty behind me, I walk.
...With beauty below me, I walk.
...With beauty above me, I walk.
...With beauty all around me, I walk.
It is finished in beauty.
It is finished in beauty.

Chapter 20

Tomas washed and waxed the car and tried to nap but he was too wired. Spirit had not yet shown up. Tomas fingered a note that he had written in Atlanta: Terry Lieber, tel. 983-2300.

What have I got to lose? He asked himself as he punched the numbers into the cordless phone pad. He was surprised when a male voice answered on the second ring.

"Terry Lieber."

"Dr. Lieber?" Tomas asked. "My name is Tomas. I was given your name by another doctor in Atlanta. I'm told that you are a first class oncologist."

Dr. Lieber spoke modestly. "Oh, I don't know. It is what I do. As to how well, I guess you would need to ask my patients."

"I have an unusual situation," Tomas began. He began to fill Dr. Lieber in on his need for a good laboratory facility in the area. He wondered if Dr. Lieber would mind meeting with him at his clinic--if nothing else, so that Tomas could see his equipment and trade information on state of the art care. Tomas trailed off uncomfortably. Maybe they were out in the middle of the desert, but a man's research lab was still sacrosanct.

Dr. Lieber was cordial, if guarded. He was curious what this man was up to. It wouldn't hurt to talk with him. He invited him to come for a visit.

"The thing is, and I hate to ask for favors like this, but I'm in a bit of a time bind. Would it be possible for me to come by sooner rather than later? Actually I've heard such fine things about you that I'm very much looking forward to meeting you."

Dr. Lieber laughed. Flattery, he thought. But he wasn't really doing anything later in the afternoon. His patient, Jim, was involved in some healing ceremony--not that it would hurt him, he supposed, but it wasn't going to cure him, either.

"I happen to have a cancellation for my last appointment today. Could you drive up this afternoon?"

Tomas leapt at the chance to get out of the trailer, even if he had just driven hundreds of miles. "Sure, thanks, I'd like that."

* * *

The stretch of road between Hidden City and Dr. Lieber's clinic passed through some of the harshest terrain in the southwest. Far off the horizon appeared layered in pastel tones: beige sand, pink and brown rock, blue sky, a stripe of white clouds. The skyline was punctuated with towering mesas. It was achingly beautiful, vast and to the untrained eye, devoid of life. But life was there. Turkey buzzards and hawks sailed the skies, lazily circling on updrafts of desert wind. Snakes and other reptiles owned the hot sand. An occasional coyote or armadillo rustled the sagebrush.

Tomas' Vanquish was soon coated with a thin layer of dust. There had been little rain here for four months, unlike the downpours that were flooding the southern states. Dust hung in the air, and despite the air conditioned interior of the car, Tomas began to feel the scratch in the back of his throat.

The scenery reminded him of some of the drives he and Spirit had taken when they visited the new house in Desert View. He missed her beside him. But he was not sorry that he had found a diversion in visiting Dr. Lieber that would keep him away from home until late at night. He wanted to be the last one to come home, not the first. He knew it was a juvenile game that he was playing, but he was still irritated with Spirit's cold shoulder routine. Two could play that game.

By the time Tomas pulled off at Dr. Lieber's facility, the temperatures were beginning to subside. The road dust and heat of the day had made him thirsty.

Dr. Lieber was coming out of his inner office and into the waiting area when Tomas walked in. There was no one else there; Tomas had noted that the parking lot was empty except for a black BMW parked near the back door.

When Tomas shook hands with Dr. Lieber he noted the doctor's curious glance at his dangling left hand. When Dr. Lieber saw that Tomas was following his glance, he quickly shifted his attention.

"Please come in," Dr. Lieber said. "We could sit in my office but it is piled with files. I'm in the middle of a lot of projects right now, so my papers are everywhere. Let's go to the staff room. Would you like a Coke?"

"Water would be fine," Tomas said. "Thank you."

There was little small talk. Neither one of the doctors had the knack for it. Instead Tomas got directly to the point: he was looking for an adequately equipped lab in order to experiment with plant material and the effect of plant material on cancerous cells.

Dr. Lieber's interest was piqued. "Do you have any certain plant material in mind" he asked.

Tomas felt foolish in his answer. "Not yet," he admitted.

"Isn't it a bit premature then to be looking for a lab?"

"I don't think so," Tomas said. "As you know the choices are few and far between out here. I would of course compensate you for the use of any equipment--I guess I would be looking to more or less rent the occasional use of your laboratory. Naturally I would give you advance notice of when I might need to look at some slides --you do have a comparison microscope, I'm sure."

Dr. Lieber nodded. "More than one, but I like one that I'm testing. Naturally it has live cell imaging chambers that control environmental variables and motorized components to automate rapid filter changes, focus and stage translation. But also a high performance incubator, high speed filter wheels, electromechanical shutters, axial focus systems and translational motorized stages. So far, I'm very impressed."

Tomas felt like he had found a compatriot who spoke a rare but precise dialect. He didn't yet want to ask to see the equipment, but he had a feeling that Dr. Lieber would not be able to resist showing him his tools.

Minutes later the two men were bent over the state of the art microscopes. Dr. Lieber showed Tomas some slide images of cells magnified and displayed on the computer monitor. Tomas was fascinated as well as highly impressed with the sophistication of the equipment. He had enjoyed good equipment when he was practicing in Atlanta, but this--was on an entirely different plane. He longed to put it to the test, to watch the cellular reactions as he subjected them to different agents. The drama of the survival or extinguishments of the basic building blocks of life: living cells.

But it was getting late. Dr. Lieber and Tomas agreed to meet again, soon. Dr. Lieber would consider Tomas' request, but was inclined to work with him. A scientist himself, he fully understood the need for the best equipment, and the breathtaking cost of it. With the right person, someone he could trust, it would be a win-win situation for both doctors.

They were finished in the lab and were making their way toward the door, through the business office when Tomas caught a glimpse of a large orange file folder inserted into a plastic vertical file holder on the secretary's desk. The slot was marked with a notecard taped to the side that read "New Patients". In large black letters on the edge of the file, Tomas saw the name: SOLEDAD, ESPIRITUD along with a sticky note that read "schedule appointment ASAP."

* * *

Tomas was a blur of confused emotion as he sped toward Hidden City. He knew one thing: he had to see what was in Spirit's file. And why and when had she been to see Dr. Lieber? His professional pride was hurt. He felt like he had caught her cheating on him with another man. I'm only her husband, he thought. Wouldn't a normal wife tell her husband if she wanted to go see another doctor? Tomas' mind was racing but one thought kept returning: did Dr. Lieber have enough information to tell Spirit the truth, the truth that Tomas had kept carefully secret for weeks? Was that why Spirit was not speaking to him?

His cell phone rang. From the number display, Tomas saw

that it was Spirit. He was tempted not to answer, but on the third ring he determined to put an end to this game of hide and seek.

He picked up. "Hello?"

"Tomas?"

"Who else?"

"Maybe the woman who answered your phone the last time I called?"

"What are you talking about?" Tomas had forgotten all about the events of his trip from Atlanta.

"Maybe you could tell me. When I called you and you were driving home from Atlanta, a woman answered your phone…"

"You must've called a wrong number." Tomas said.

"No, I didn't. The woman said that you were in the motel office. I naturally took that to mean that you were in a motel office checking into the motel."

Oh, Jesus, Tomas thought.

"I just haven't had a chance to tell you about that, Spirit. Honest to God, nothing happened. It was not what you thought." *Why didn't that girl tell me that someone called?*

"So what was it, Tomas?"

"It was nothing." He proceeded to tell her the whole story of the stranded vehicle, the dead battery, the closed road. "I'm sorry, honey, that I upset you. I love you, Spirit. I'm not going to do anything to wreck what I've waited so long to create. Do you believe me?"

"I feel like an idiot."

"It's okay, and I'm sorry that I didn't tell you sooner. I didn't want to upset you, and truly, it was nothing."

"Where are you now, Tomas? I've been at home for a while. I was up at Clara and Bonnie's house at the healing."

"I wondered where you were. How is your arm?" He wanted to change the subject.

"It aches some, but I don't want to take any painkillers yet. They put me to sleep and might affect the baby."

"I'll be back in a little while."

"Tomas, I don't think that the healing is working. The sing

is still going on, but I'm wondering if Jim is even still alive. Clara feels the same way."

Tomas thought it over. He didn't know the family well, but it seemed that the healer would know what to do. From what he had heard about Jim's failing health, death would not be an unexpected event. He and Spirit had their own problems. He wanted to leave it alone.

"What would you have me do, Spirit?"

"Well, you're a doctor. Maybe he is still alive, and needs more than sand painting healing. Maybe tomorrow you could go with me to the sing. To just take a look at him, if the family wants you to? I would feel better knowing what you think."

"Is that why you went to see Dr. Lieber? Because you trusted what I think?" Tomas said pointedly. Now it was her turn to explain.

Spirit fell silent. How had he found out?

Chapter 21

Dan Weatherford stopped by Hank's room at the hospital long enough for the doctor to let him know that Hank had dodged a bullet. The clogged artery was a widow maker, and the other vessels were badly damaged. "He is alive, for now," was the best the doctor would venture. He looked exhausted, like he had been on his feet for half his lifetime. Dan understood. Sometimes he felt the same.

"Now it's in God's hands," said the nurse.

Dan looked at her and said, "Is he awake?"

"Sort of. He's on a morphine drip, so he's in and out."

"May I see him?"

"Let me check with him."

Hank was high on the morphine when Dan walked into the room. "You've had a busy couple of days," said Dan.

"You got that right. How about you, old man? Holding down the fort? Keeping the bad guys under control?"

"Well my biggest problem is, my wife doesn't understand why I'm never home."

Hank laughed. "Welcome to the club, bud. But if she's complaining, you're still married. When she stops complaining and starts walking around like a bow-legged cowgirl, you've got problems."

Dan knew the story of Hank's divorce. By heart. "I don't think I want to be in the divorce club, Hank. I just stopped by to check on you. The only news is the sing for Jim Hammer is going on."

Hank interrupted. "How's Bonnie taking it?"

"Not too well. She goes up and down between taking care

of people and crying hysterically."

Dan was about to tell Hank about Spirit and how she fell and broke her arm when Hank interrupted.

"What about that file I gave you?" Hank was not tracking. It seemed to Dan that he was about to go back to sleep.

"I don't understand what it is that you want me to do. What does it mean?"

"I figured that Cal Kingman would have called you by now. Kingman Brick has been good to me over the years, Dan, if you know what I mean."

"No, Hank, I don't know what you mean."

"Well, Goddamnit, Dan, you need to learn the system. I'm trying to do you a favor here, and teach you, but I swear it is like talking to a choirboy."

Dan was mystified. "Sprite said it looked like some kind of code..."

"Sprite? The lawyer? *Geezuz Dan,* did you show it to her?"

Dan wanted to hide. He knew by Hank's tone that he had screwed up, he just didn't know how.

"All right, I'll spell it out for you..." and the old sheriff started, "when I was just starting out, it was, it was...it was, different..."

Dan listened and watched as he drifted off, breathing slower, until he slept.

Chapter 22

Morning came to the Hidden City in a golden haze of sunlight. The Chicken Coop began to fill up with its regular customers who gathered as faithfully as the early attenders of mass at the old Catholic Church near the town center. The talk that morning was of the healing for Jim Hammer--how Hosteen Clah III had failed and how Jim, a regular Saturday customer, was dead. Two customers had been at the sing most of the night. They described the argument that erupted between Hosteen Clah III and Jim's daughter, Bonnie.

Bonnie had been up for at least three days without any sleep at all. In that time, people said, she became more and more bizarre in her words. She spoke faster and faster to the guests. They could not get a word in. If they tried she snapped at them. This was not the Bonnie whom everyone knew but rather a witch, it seemed, the way her laughter became a cackle or a shriek or something in between. Others saw her sitting on the bed in her father's bedroom, rocking back and forth and laughing hysterically. Had she become possessed? They whispered and kept a cautious watch. One neighbor took her by the arm and tried to get her to eat something. Bonnie pushed her away, hissing obscenities. The neighbor slipped out the door and went to find Clara to tell her that Bonnie was *cracking up.*

Clara nodded and went to the main house. She checked on Clay, her grandson, who was sleeping peacefully in his pullout bed. Bonnie was at the sink, gulping water directly from the kitchen faucet. The water was pouring from her cupped hand, some into her mouth, but more spilling onto the front of her plaid shirt. She was drenched, but seemed oblivious to her wild appearance.

"Bonnie, come to the hogan," Clara said calmly.

When Bonnie raised her head from the faucet and looked at her mother, Clara knew that the neighbor was right: Bonnie was not there, in those eyes and in her motions she had gone. Clara put her arms around her daughter and whispered into her ear, saying "It's okay honey, I'm here. Come with me now, it is time to say goodbye to your father." Bonnie slumped against her mother and began to cry loudly, wailing and protesting that only she could save her father, that the shaman was a goddamn fake.

Clara hushed her and used a kitchen towel to mop the water off of her face and neck. "Come on, Bonnie. Let's go." As they were leaving the kitchen Clara asked her sister, who was making more coffee for the crowd, to call Sprite Soledad and ask her to come right away--that Bonnie was sick in the head and that Jim was dying or dead--to just get there and bring Tomas with her. Their home telephone number was taped to the wall by the telephone. Her sister nodded.

Bonnie let her mother take her to the hogan. Hosteen Clah III allowed them to come in. During the night he had examined Jim's body and had found the dark blue and purple marks on the inside of his arm. Some areas were yellowing, from previous punctures. Hosteen Clah III had swaddled Jim's body but left his arm out to show Clara and Bonnie. The healer was angry. He had not failed, this man had died because someone had put needles in his arms. Maybe it was Jim himself, the healer said. Was he a drug addict?

Bonnie lunged for the healer, nearly knocking him over. "My father was no junkie," she screamed in Hosteen Clah III's face. That doctor he was seeing, so secretively--he must have done this to him.

The healer looked at Clara in confusion. Clara's face had paled and she looked helplessly down at Jim's swollen and bruised arm, then at Bonnie, whose eyes had turned into black holes and were beginning to move back and forth very fast as she began to pace and mutter and pull the air with her curled fingers.

Clara had never seen anyone behave like her daughter, but Hosteen Clah III had. He had been called on more than one occasion to homes of family members whose son or daughter, wife or husband, had started acting just this way. Sometimes they got better and sometimes they didn't. Some simply disappeared from the community and came back weeks later, heavy with medication.

But Hosteen Clah III could not pay attention to Bonnie right now. He tried to persuade Bonnie to leave. He needed to conclude the ceremony. The final dancers were coming, he could hear them approaching and knew that they would be dressed to emulate certain holy spirits. They would dance nearby and then depart one by one, taking the illness of the patient away with them. The sand paintings would be ritually destroyed. There was work to be done even after death.

Bonnie had to be pulled from her father's side by Clara and the shaman. She had a new strength, and Clara was afraid that they would not be able to take her out even with both of them pulling. The crowd was in place outside, singing and praising the gods, thanking them and Bonnie suddenly broke free and rushed those who were closest to the hogan. She slapped one of her uncles and pushed her way out of the circle. They let her pass, thinking she just needed to blow off steam. She went in the house and slammed the door behind her. Later they heard her slam the door to her old Chevy and gun the engine. She threw gravel with the tires as she spun out onto the main road, heading toward Hidden City.

Clara was worried but had to attend to Jim just then. The circle of friends and families, singers and dancers, closed and there was silence as the shaman announced that his magic was not able to work because Jim was too far gone before the healer had arrived. The poison was strong, he had taken it in through his arms. The people murmured anxiously. They had never known a patient to die during a healing, what was this? Hosteen Clah III had never lost a patient in such a public way either, and he hung his head in humiliation and privately wondered if his powers had flown away.

The crowd dissipated in the predawn hours. By the time Sprite and Tomas arrived, only a few close family members sat with Clara and the fuming shaman. They were gathered in the kitchen. Jim's body was still wrapped in blankets in the ceremonial hogan. Tomas excused himself to Clara after he asked her permission to take a look at Jim. She nodded. The shaman turned away.

Tomas examined Jim's body and noted he likely had been dead for more than just a few hours. Tomas returned to the kitchen and sat with Clara, Sprite, and Hosteen Clah III. Tomas gently questioned Clara about the marks on her husband's arms. He was surprised when she told him that Jim had been going to see a doctor, Doctor Lieber, and that he would have the marks on his arms when he returned from the appointments.

Tomas surmised from Clara's explanations and from Jim's emaciated state that he had cancer. Clara agreed.

"Jim told me that the doctor said he got it from working at the brick factory years ago and had breathed in poisons in the dust. Dr. Lieber gave Jim vitamins or something, to make his system stronger," Clara explained.

"I think I'm going to make a trip to see Dr. Lieber. I'll call first, and let him know about Jim. Clara, is that okay with you?"

"Of course. But what about Bonnie?"

"I haven't seen her. Probably she is just off driving around. Some people need time to adjust and want to be alone. Others need to have family by them and can't stand to be alone," Tomas said.

"Bonnie was not herself when she left," said Clara. "I've never seen her like that. In fact I have never seen anyone act like that." Hosteen Clah III nodded in agreement.

"I think she is possessed by evil spirits," the healer said. "We need to find her."

Tomas concurred but he had a separate agenda. He wanted to see Dr. Lieber about his lab, to be sure, but he also wanted to find out what Dr. Lieber had told Spirit. Spirit herself was closemouthed on the subject at first. In a conversation that had gone on long into the night, she admitted that she had gone to see Dr. Lieber because she feared that Tomas was not telling her the whole truth about her condition. She had wanted a second opinion, but she didn't want to hurt Tomas' feelings by telling him that she was going to go see Dr. Lieber. It was her body, after all.

Tomas had heatedly pointed out that it might be her body, but it was his child too, and he had every right to know anything that might affect the child. Spirit agreed, and apologized for not taking that fact into consideration. Around two in the morning, there was forgiveness. They had made love and fallen asleep exhausted only to be awakened by a telephone call. Jim Hammer was dead.

* * *

Bonnie grabbed her car keys and purse and was headed for the door when she saw her Dad's Smith & Wesson revolver laying on his bedside table. On an impulse she took it, not knowing why, only knowing that it was comforting. It had been a part of her image of her father for as long as she could remember. A dark place inside her toyed with the idea of using the gun on herself. But she couldn't do that, at least not here and not now. She was trying to make sense of everything but bits and pieces of normal kept breaking off and running away. She tried hard to bring the pieces back together but couldn't.

She kept seeing her father's thin body and that terrible arm-- what had he been doing? What had his doctor been doing? Why hadn't she seen the ruined arm before?

Bonnie raced to Hidden City, watching the speedometer climb to the accustomed fifty-five, then sixty then higher and higher as Bonnie watched the needle as if from a distance. It had nothing to do with her; she was invincible, flying, an avenger of her father.

Out of habit she pulled into the Coroner's Office parking lot. She had little recollection of time and scenery passing between her home and the office. She had her keys; it was a simple matter to let herself in. There, she was at work. It was just another ordinary day, after all. Nothing had happened. Her father was not dead. The shaman had not screwed up. She had gotten what she had saved and scraped together and borrowed and paid for: a beautiful, nine day healing. Her father would wake up soon, and get up, and walk away. Bonnie would help him into his own bed and take care of him, feeding him corn pudding and spicy beef until he filled out those scarecrow clothes he had been wearing lately.

On her desk she saw the stack of death certificates that she had been researching for Dan. She needed to do something with those...what was it? She looked through the stack and was drawn to the signature: Dr. Terry Lieber. Again and again, Dr. Terry Lieber. Suddenly it struck her: Dr. Lieber had not been treating all those people. He had been killing them, one by one. And now he had killed her father.

Her writhing brain calmed with a purpose. A design formed. She began to lay out the death certificates in a star pattern, for the star would lead her to justice. It would point out the way to Dr. Lieber, and another way, for her own escape and safety.

Only she knew the truth. It was up to her now, almost like God himself had given her the right and the responsibility to find this Dr. Lieber and stop him. She was overwhelmed by her discovery--it made perfect sense in her estranged mind. She put her head down on her desk. Her body was so tired, so weary of work and mothering, trying to pay the bills, to cook food. And now with no father to count on for help. She wept, but she could not sleep. She had to go on. She had to find Dr. Lieber.

One gun might not be enough, thought Bonnie. She used her key to the Sheriff's private office and started looking. There, in the drawer, was a Smith & Wesson revolver. Funny how both of them liked the same kind of gun, Bonnie thought. The idea began to strike her as incredibly funny. She began to giggle, then to sing a song that she made up on the spot, to the old tune of *Pop Goes the Weasel*:

Round and round

The red fox chased the doctor,
The doctor thought it was great fun,
POP goes the doctor...

"Oh my God I'm hilarious," shrieked Bonnie. In the car she tried to stuff the Sheriff's gun into her purse, but found there was already a gun there. She wiped her laughing tears from her face and pondered how the other gun had got there. That was funny too, wasn't it? She collapsed in laughter against the car's steering wheel. But soon she pulled herself together. She had a job to do. Bonnie floored the accelerator and blew through town, never stopping once at a stop light or stop sign.

* * *

Dan Weatherford tossed and turned and mumbled in his sleep. As a result his wife could not rest either, and by morning she had had it; she took her pillow and a blanket to the vinyl covered Lazy-Boy recliner in the family room and made a nest. The kids would not be awake for another half hour so she could at least get in a short nap.

She wondered what it was that was causing Dan to sleep so poorly, then put her concern out of her mind. Whatever it was, she needed some sleep.

When his wife climbed out of bed in a grumpy huff, Dan gave up on trying to sleep and opted for a hot shower before he made his own coffee. He always had just one quick cup at home then two or three more when he stopped by the Coop before going to work.

Dan had just lathered up his thinning hair when he heard the telephone ring. Shoot, he thought. His wife would have to pick up and she was in no mood. He felt sorry for whoever was on the other end of the phone conversation. By the time he had finished his shower Pauline had lit her first cigarette and was waiting for him. She didn't look happy.

"You need to call that lawyer --Sprite Soledad," she snapped.

"Okay, thanks, honey. I'm sorry that the phone woke you up."

"What does she want with you?" his wife demanded.

"Well, I don't know. But it must be important if she called me here. She wouldn't do that for no reason."

His wife was jealous of any woman who paid any attention to Dan. Dan thought when they were younger that she just watched too much television. All those soap operas gave her goofy ideas. He figured that it would pass; he never intentionally gave her any reason to doubt his faithfulness to her. But over the years she seemed to grow more jealous. When Bonnie came to work part time at his office she threw what could only be called a temper tantrum. She refused to speak with him for two days, and accused him of requesting that Bonnie be assigned to their office. Dan had given up on trying to reason with his wife and at some point just began to ignore her jabs. And began to spend more and more time at work.

Dan called Sprite back from his cell phone after he had pulled out of the driveway and was headed for the office.

"Thanks for calling back, Dan." Sprite said. "I have sad news. Jim passed away during the first ritual."

"Oh, wow. That's terrible. How's Bonnie?"

"Bonnie took off, Dan. That's why I'm calling you, actually. People said she tore out of here in her car, early, after acting wild toward the healer and some other people. Of course she hadn't slept in days. But she shouldn't be driving, in any event. Are you on your way to the office?"

"Yes. I'll be there in a few minutes. If Bonnie is there I'll take her home and make sure that she goes to bed."

"Tomas could give her a sleeping pill if she can't relax. You know how it is."

"I sure do. I didn't sleep well last night either. That reminds me, we need to talk about that Kingman file. Hank told me something the last time I saw him that has me worried. Are you going to be around today, at your office?"

"I will be if you need to see me. It is starting to sound like nobody got much sleep last night. What time will you stop by?"

"Maybe we could just grab some lunch at the Coop? "

"That sounds good. Do I need to go up to Clara's?"

"I'll let you know if they need you. I'll check in again soon."

"Okay, thanks. I've got a lot of work to do at the office, but I'm there if you need me."

"I'll see you at lunch then. Bye."

Dan ended the call just as he pulled in to the parking lot at work. Bonnie's car was nowhere to be seen. He wouldn't blame her for not working today, heck, her dad had just died. She would probably call in as soon as the office opened. He wasn't worried about Bonnie. She wasn't the type to do anything crazy.

Chapter 23

Sprite was trying to eat an egg salad sandwich one-handed. She was still getting used to having the cast and sling on her left arm. The simple act of picking up a sandwich and getting it to her mouth without spilling large chunks of it, was daunting.

Dan ate heartily with two hands wrapped around a large breast of fried chicken. His appetite was rarely affected by the stress of his job or the stress of his marriage, and he never gained weight. Sprite envied him. She loved to eat, but it seemed to show up immediately on her, especially now that she was slowed in her activities by the pregnancy. She couldn't wait to get back on her bicycle in the spring.

Dan produced the Kingman Brick Company file and laid it on the table. Sprite picked it up and thumbed through it again. She was not used to having only one working hand. She looked at Dan and raised her eyebrows.

"And?" she said.

Dan fidgeted with his napkins, folding it and opening it and refolding it again. "I asked Hank about this," he began. "I told him I showed it to you and I think he would have jumped out of his bed if he hadn't been hooked up to all the equipment. He was half out of his mind with the morphine."

"And the other half?"

"Still working, still Hank. He was trying to help me, in his own way. And trying to help out Cal Kingman too. He said he thought Kingman would have called me by now."

"About what?"

"I'm not sure--maybe the project that we--Bonnie and I-- were working on. It has to do with giving a report about the number of people who have died of cancer around here in the past few years. Kingman has to file a report with the state board of health, or one of those state agencies."

"Oh, okay. Did he say anything else?"

Dan appeared embarrassed. "He said he was trying to teach me how things really worked in politics. Like if I'm going to be the sheriff someday I need to know something. He called me...a choirboy."

Sprite put down her sandwich and picked up her coffee cup. "So what do you think he meant?" She had her own ideas, looking at the stack of cards and letters in the file.

"I'm not as dumb as I must look, Sprite. Especially after seeing what my old partner Tiny Lucas was into when he was still alive. I guess he took money from just about anyone that he could shake down." Dan suddenly looked older, his face more lined.

He went on. "I keep my nose clean, but I see things going on, I hear about things. I guess I should report some of what I hear to someone, but I'm not sure who that would be. I'm not so sure what would happen if I went to a judge or the state's attorney office, or even higher up. I like my job and I do want to be sheriff someday. What if I ended up being the butt of the joke?"

Sprite listened seriously. Dan was right, it wasn't safe to assume that just because one is in the right, that justice will be done. It was sad, but true. But she loved that he was not a part of the jaundiced system. Maybe together they could help improve the situation so that one could count a little more on justice, a little less on money to make the world go around.

"Take it easy, Dan," she said. "There's a judge here that runs a tight ship. Remember him from when Tiny Lucas and Lisa tried to frame Tomas? If there is something shaky going on with Kingman Brick Company, we could go to him. He could put some pressure on the State's Attorney to look into the case.

"I can't. Not if it would involve Hank. I can't go against Hank, Sprite."

Sprite pressed her lips together. "I can understand that. He has practically raised you. Let me think about it a little, Dan. Maybe I can help."

The more Sprite thought about the implications of what Hank had told Dan the more upset and depressed she became. And the more determined to do something about it. She asked Dan if she could take the Kingman file with her. He hesitated, then thought he might as well allow it, she had seen it before. Some part of him also wanted to get to the bottom of the Kingman situation and if there was any kind of corruption going on, to put a stop to it somehow. People needed to be able to trust the Sheriff's office to be honest and law abiding, Dan thought. Even if it costs me my job.

Chapter 24

Gigi had no intention of being a waitress her whole life. She knew that she was pretty. All she had to do was to look in the mirror, which she did as often as she could, and see that her hair was shiny, blonde, and hung halfway down her back in a smooth curtain, to know that. One reason she did like being a waitress was there was that long, tall mirror behind the counter where the coffee maker stood, where she could see herself every time that she pulled a chalky mug out of the stack of plastic dishwasher racks.

Usually she saw not only herself but Possum, the dishwasher. He liked to look at her and even if he smelled bad, she kind of liked his attention. Gigi thought if Possum would just pay some attention to his appearance he wouldn't be that bad looking. One time when things were slow at the counter, and Possum was sitting during his break, Gigi told him that she thought he would look cool with some blonde streaks in his hair. Possum blushed but all day he thought about it. She wouldn't let it go, either.

About a week or so later, Gigi brought in a couple of magazines about movie stars. She waited until Possum sat down late in the afternoon but before the supper crowd began to build, then she pulled the magazines out from behind the counter and showed him where she had turned the corners of the pages down. On every page there was a guy with much shorter hair than his, with blond streaks or in some pictures just the end of the hair in front, with the hair sticking straight up in front.

"Spikes," Gigi said, "That's what you need. Don't they look cool?"

Possum looked but he was not able to concentrate. He noticed instead the tiny blond hair on her tanned forearms and the smell of her--something so sweet--and he breathed deeper, trying to trap that smell inside himself. He couldn't think of a thing to say; he grinned and could feel himself growing red in the face.

Gigi was holding the magazine up near his face and was looking first at the magazine and then at him. "I bet I could make you look just like that," she said.

Possum found his words. "I wouldn't mind."

"You would have to come to my house when my parents aren't home," she said, "I would wash your hair and cut it first, then we could bleach the ends. I could get the stuff I need from the beauty school supply store after the next time I get paid."

Possum couldn't believe that Gigi was willing to spend time with him and was inviting him to her house. It was the happiest day of his life, he thought. She could have told him that she thought it would be a good idea to shave his head, or give him a home tattoo, and he would have said, "yeah, that's good, go on and do it"--even if it hurt or burned or bled.

Nick's head popped into view in the square pass-through cut into the back wall, "Possum, get back to work. Break time is over, and I need for you to get more chicken out of the walk-in. Gigi, wipe down that counter again. I can see some places that you missed, get those crumbs at the far end. Then make sure the ketchup bottles are filled and washed off at each table."

Gigi rolled her blue eyes and Possum laughed like it was the funniest thing he had ever seen. "He needs to get a life," she whispered dramatically.

Possum felt cozy, with Gigi whispering just to him.

* * *

Dr. Lieber was at his computer, writing up the results from the last treatment he had given Jim. He was only somewhat uneasy about the speed of the intravenous infusion. In his view it could be seen as an understandable and anticipated move to clear toxins from Jim's liver. What he didn't write--what he would never write--was that he pushed the envelope on Jim. At the time he thought that it didn't matter, the man was going to die no matter what he did, and if the procedure killed him, well, it may have also saved him the prolonged agony of a slower death. And he hadn't died, had he? No harm, no foul.

Terry Lieber's clinic was closed that day. He gave himself one day a week to catch up on paperwork, to clean, to be in the lab with only Verdi on the CD player. Telephones rang, but went to the answering machine. His secretary would pick up the calls the next day.

Outside on the highway there was the occasional zing of a car or truck rushing past at the speed limit. It was all background noise to Dr. Lieber as he hunched over his monitor's screen, the mouse in his right hand, a cup of coffee in his left. He had left the inner doors of the clinic open–front and back, to get some airflow through the building on this cool and breezy day.

He heard the car enter the gravel drive. The tires struck a single stone in such a way that it pinged and clattered across the drive. In the remaining silence, it was like a single pistol shot.

He looked up, but the car had passed his line of vision. A moment later he heard a car engine sound around back. *Probably someone who forgot that the office is closed today,* he thought. Terry Lieber hoisted his tall frame out of the desk chair, and picked up his coffee cup to drop it off back in the kitchen on his way to the door.

Looking out the back window, he still could see only a patch of the parking lot in the rear. But the car motor had been killed, and he thought he could hear footsteps, then a small cough, of a person walking outside the building. He moved to the doorway to get a better view of the lot and to head off whoever would want to come in, and saw an older model Chevrolet--it looked like a Cavalier--that badly needed washing. Whoever it was must have come down some dusty back roads, judging from the red dirt caked up under the wheel wells.

The front screen door opened and shut.

Dr. Lieber turned and walked down the short hallway that

led to the reception area. A wild eyed woman stood just inside the front door. She saw him at the same time that he saw her and they both stopped still for a half second.

"The office is closed," began Dr. Lieber. He didn't recognize her as a patient. And yet it was clear that she needed medical help. She held her large purse close to her side, clamped shut with her right elbow.

"Good," she said. "Are you the doctor?"

"Yes, I'm Terry Lieber. May I help you with something? Are you feeling okay?"

She said nothing but only stared at him with those empty eyes. She was there and yet not all there. Dr. Lieber walked between her and the secretary's desk, suddenly wanting to be near a telephone. He wasn't sure if this woman was dangerous but there was definitely something out of the ordinary. He quickly reached under the edge of the desk and pushed a red button. He was glad he had invested in the security alarm system that would alert police to an emergency at the clinic. Just as he straightened and turned to face Bonnie, she spoke.

"You killed my dad."

He couldn't make sense of it. She was reaching with her left hand into the soft worn leather bag that hung from her right shoulder from a strap. She drew out a gun and wave it at his face.

"Wait a second. I think you're mistaken. I'm a doctor. I didn't kill anyone. Who are you?"

"I'm Bonnie Hammer. My dad was Jim Hammer. He died."

Dr. Lieber's stomach clenched. "I'm so sorry to hear about your father. He was a good man, but he was very sick, you know."

"The medicine man showed me his arm. He said it was the drugs that killed him." The gun was still pointed directly at his face.

"Look, I tried to help your dad. The medicine that I was giving him didn't kill him--he had cancer and he had it bad. He was going to die no matter what."

Tears filled Bonnie's eyes and spilled over, ran down both

cheeks. "Hosteen Clah III can heal anyone. He's the best shaman around and I paid him a lot of money to cure my dad…"

Terry Lieber rolled his eyes. "You people with your magic. When are you going to give up on that dancing around and shaking sticks at the evil spirits? You might as well wave a magic wand."

Bonnie raised the barrel of the Smith & Wesson by an inch and sighted on Dr. Lieber's nose. "Here's my magic wand. It will make you -"

Bonnie collapsed on the floor, unconscious.

* * *

When Bonnie came to, she was wedged between the steering wheel of her Cavalier and the driver's seat. She raised her head and listened to the sound of the wind pushing against the car. She reached for her bag and tried to clear her head. How did she get in her car? Bonnie remembered nothing except pulling a gun on Dr. Lieber. But that was inside the clinic. She was surprised to find two guns – and wondered what she had done.

Gunning the engine, Bonnie threw gravel again as she pulled out of the clinic driveway and took off.

* * *

Tomas was anxious to get to the Lieber's lab. He needed to know what was in his wife's file, but now he was also curious to know what the doctor had done to Jim Hammer. He knew that he should rest some but his mind would not give him peace until he had some answers. Spirit was preoccupied with trying to find Bonnie --no one had seen her all day, and she had failed to show up at work. Her child, Clay, was well cared for by his grandmother, but if Bonnie had not returned by nightfall he was going to start fussing for his mother.

Tomas wasn't sure he should leave Spirit by herself for too long. She'd been having some cramping ever since her fall up at the new house. With her broken arm, she really needed to rest, eat well, and try to relax but instead she had not slept, had no appetite and now seemed intent on tracking down Bonnie. Tomas knew that Spirit pushed herself when others needed her. He wanted to remind her that their baby needed her now more than anyone else, and she needed to slow down.

At least she was taking the time to eat lunch with Dan Weatherford. Tomas liked Dan's calm demeanor and knew that it would help Spirit to slow down her pace. He had been invited to join them, but right now Tomas was anxious to get on the road so that he could be back that evening. Spirit gave him her solemn promise that she would have a solid meal, then go home and take a nap. Dan Weatherford was just as eager to find Bonnie--after all, she worked for his office--and Spirit could leave that responsibility to him. "Doctor's orders," Tomas told Spirit.

She made a face and then smiled at him. She was happy that they were back to being easy with one another. She believed Tomas' explanation of the woman's voice on his cell phone. They had made up. Tomas was still not quite settled down from Spirit's visit to Dr. Lieber, but that would fall into place as well.

After lunch with Dan Weatherford, Sprite took the Kingman Brick Company file and went to her office. The message light was blinking. She listened: two messages, both from Clara. Had she found Bonnie, or heard from her? Sprite could hear Clay whining in the background, and the voices of women saying ssshhh, grandmother is on the phone.

Sprite smiled tiredly and thought of her own baby. Sprite moved from her office desk chair to a softer, upholstered recliner that Tomas had bought for her when they first found out that she was pregnant. She pulled two throw pillows from the floor beside the chair, and put one under her calves; one at the small of her back. She opened the Kingman file again and began to read. Before she had reached the second note, her eyes closed. Within seconds, she was asleep.

Seventy miles away Tomas pulled the Vanquish off the highway and into the gravel lot. He parked in the same spot - next to Dr. Lieber's BMW behind the office building. Suddenly his phone rang. The display showed a call from his associate Frank in Atlanta.

"Buddy, what's up? I'm in kind of a hurry here."

"Bad news, but I'll keep it brief. That talk about Terry Lieber stirring up trouble for mining companies? You won't believe it, but he is stirring up trouble for you and me too."

Tomas closed his eyes. His dealings with Frank and their backers had to be kept secret. If Lieber was snooping into their business, he needed to stop.

Tomas saw that the back door to Lieber's building was open and decided to go in. As he ended the call he realized that while he was on the phone, another car had arrived; he had heard tires on gravel.

He called out loudly as he stepped in, saying "Hello? Terry?"

There was no answer. The office building echoed with his words.

"He's probably in the lab," Tomas said. He walked around the reception area and headed toward the lab. As soon as he pushed the door open he knew that Dr. Lieber was not in the lab, it was too dark inside. "Hello?" he said anyway. No answer.

Tomas turned. He neared the small alcove that held the reception desk, filing cabinets and computers he heard voices, a woman, loud and heated, and Dr. Lieber.

Tomas then saw Bonnie, sweaty and crying, pointing a gun at the doctor.

Then, in a dead faint, she hit the floor.

* * *

Tomas grabbed the gun from Bonnie. He spun and pulled the trigger, once, twice, three times. Dr. Lieber crashed to the floor.

* * *

Tomas realized that he had time to do what he had come to do. Tomas found and removed his wife's file. He scanned the three pages: one for file setup including insurance information, contact information, assessment coding. Page two was a sheet for the appointment notes. Tomas saw the ragged handwriting stating a brief history, notable past medical issues, references to the ob/gyn who had been following Spirit's obstetric care, and the information given by Spirit as to the tumor that had been detected. Third page was a copy of an order for lab tests. Tomas looked at the boxes that had been checked off. Most were standard: blood panels for hemoglobin levels, sedimentation rates, and so on. Then Tomas saw a note that was not at all standard. In Dr. Lieber's handwriting, underlined, was a simple three word statement: Consider accelerated chelation.

Drops of sweat formed on Tomas' forehead. Jesus Christ, he thought, what could the man have been thinking? He deserved to die.

He took the file to his car and hid it beneath the seat. Quickly, he dragged Bonnie's unconscious body outside and shoved her into the driver's seat of her car. He shoved the gun into Bonnie's bag.

Tomas ran his fingers through his stubble of hair and straightened his clothing.

* * *

He opened the door for Marcus Steamer and pointed in the direction of Dr. Terry Lieber's body. A deputy from the Reservation police followed. Tomas guessed there would be many more people arriving very soon. Detective Steamer asked Tomas not to leave. "We'll be asking you a few questions," said Chief Steamer.

I'll bet, thought Tomas.

Chapter 25

Clara and her sisters entertained Clay and kept him distracted while the surreal day passed by. Jim's thin body was taken to the Coroner's office. Clara had a horrifying moment when she realized that Bonnie might encounter her father's body at her workplace, if that was where she had gone. But Dan Weatherford assured her that all precautions would be taken to spare Bonnie that cruel scene. Dan himself had talked with the Coroner about the need for an autopsy after Tomas Hotone called him to suggest it might be necessary.

Dan Weatherford wasn't sure where Tomas was coming from. Jim's death had not raised suspicions in his mind. But Tomas said he had come across some information at Dr. Lieber's office that involved his treatment methods for Jim, so a toxicology report might be very useful. Dan passed that opinion along to the Coroner, who agreed. The results, though, might take a while. The last time he had sent out for a toxicology report it had taken a month to get anything back from the lab in Flagstaff. Tomas specified that the blood tests needed to identify calcium and potassium levels. Dan wrote it down.

The coroner changed the subject. "Have you seen Bonnie? She hasn't called in, even to let us know about her dad."

"No, I know. She is usually so conscientious, too. She didn't call me, and as far as I can tell she hasn't come by the Sheriff's office. I figure she is just too upset. Probably holed up somewhere at a girlfriend's house, crying her eyes out, poor kid."

"Yeah, that sounds right. Speaking of the Sheriff, how is Hank doing?"

"He was doing pretty well but then he developed an infection after the heart surgery. His temperature is way up. I'll drop in to see him tonight if he is awake, otherwise tomorrow. I want to tell him about Jim, and now Dr. Lieber."

"What about Dr. Lieber?"

Dan realized that he didn't know yet. "Oh, wow, yeah, this just happened. Somebody shot Terry Lieber in his office. I got a call from Tomas Hotone; he discovered the body when he went there to meet with Dr. Lieber. I contacted Marcus Steamer--the clinic is technically on Reservation land--and I'm waiting to hear more."

The coroner was surprised. "Shot? Was it a robbery, or what?"

Dan said that they didn't know much yet except the clinic was closed today like it was every Wednesday. So maybe it was someone who knew that there wouldn't be anyone around and had been looking for drugs, or money, or both. Maybe Dr. Lieber had surprised the intruder, and had been killed so that he would not be able to identify the person. Like the occasional knock-off of a Quikmart, or gas station, nothing personal.

"Will I be getting another body?" asked the coroner.

"I don't think so. You know that the tribal police have their own coroner and morgue. Marcus may be calling me to help him out with one thing or another--we talk back and forth, you know, when something big comes up."

"Well I hope they catch the son of a bitch who killed him. Those people don't have any doctors to spare up there. I've heard he was a real go-getter about the environment. He's been after the mining companies about the way they expose their workers to radiation."

"Yeah, that's what I hear."

"Okay, I've got to go. Say, if Bonnie shows up, have her give me a call."

"Sure, and if you hear from her make sure that she gets in touch with me."

* * *

Cal Kingman had a problem. He needed help from Sheriff Andrews. Things were heating up with the state's investigation into the cancer deaths of former miners. He had just ignored the third phone message from one of the state EPA attorneys, asking for his data. Cal punched in the Sheriff's telephone number and waited for someone to pick up.

Dan Weatherford heard the Sheriff's private line ringing. The receptionist was away from her desk, so after four rings Dan made it to the telephone and answered the call.

"Sheriff Andrew's desk."

"Hank? Is that you?"

"No, this is Deputy Dan Weatherford."

"Is the Sheriff in?"

"No, sorry he is not. May I take a message?"

"This is Cal Kingman."

It took a second and then Dan registered the name. Kingman Brick Company.

"Oh, Hank said that you would be calling. I'm sorry to tell you that he is in the hospital. He had a heart attack. He had to have a quadruple bypass. But he made it through."

Cal Kingman held his breath. He could feel his own heartbeat quicken at this news. "How long do you think he'll be out of the office?" he asked.

"Looks like it could be quite a while. He did talk to me about you, though. Gave me his file and said to help you out, that you would be calling."

Kingman breathed out. It wasn't great, but it was something. "Maybe we should get together then, and talk face to face." He wanted to get to know this new man. He had worked together well with Hank Andrews for a very long time, but no one lives forever. If Hank thought that his deputy would be a good choice for him to work with, then he would give it a try.

The deputy agreed. He had some questions for Cal Kingman. And he was sure that Sprite would want to get to know him too.

"I'll come to Hidden City next week if you would like. How

is Monday for you?"

"I'll have to get back with you. Tuesday might be better. We had a couple of deaths around here in the last couple of days. Monday will probably be the funerals - – at least for Dr. Lieber."

Again Cal Kingman held his breath. "Dr. Lieber? Dr. Terry Lieber."

"Oh, you know him?"

It had to be the same doctor that was pushing the EPA to go after the mining industry. "Was he a cancer doctor that works up on the Reservation past the First Mesa?"

'That would be him. He was shot yesterday. In his office."

"That's --that's terrible. Who did it?"

"Not sure yet. The Reservation police are investigating, not our office."

"You never know, do you? A man like him--doctor...Jesus.
"

Dan knew what he was feeling. "We never do know, I guess, when our number is going to be pulled."

The main phone line began to ring, and Dan begged off the conversation with Cal Kingman. "I'll let you know when the funeral will be. If you can come here then we can talk about your situation. You'll have to fill me in from the beginning, unless the Sheriff starts feeling better. He sleeps a lot right now and is on some heavy medicine."

"I'll come down, and I'll visit Hank too. Give him my best. Nice talking with you. I appreciate it."

"No problem," said Dan. "Talk to you later."

* * *

In the heat of activity at Dr. Lieber's office, Tomas had forgoten to call Spirit to let her know what had happened. He was going to be very late getting home. As much as he preferred to talk in person, he had to call to let her know when to expect him and to make sure that she had gotten some rest.

He dialed the home number and waited for her to pick up. The telephone rang for the requisite number of times, and then went to the answering machine. Tomas wondered why she hadn't picked up; the telephone was right next to the bed and she could easily have reached for it even if she had been resting in bed. The ring tone was so loud that there was no way that she could sleep through it. What was going on?

Tomas interrupted Marcus Steamer long enough to say that he needed to get home. "My wife is pregnant and not feeling well," Tomas explained. "Why don't I just leave you my home and cell phone numbers so that you can call me if you need to ask me any questions?"

Marcus thought for a moment and decided he could trust Tomas to be available when they needed him. After all, he was the one who called in the incident. It didn't rule out that he had also been the one to shoot Dr. Lieber, but the chances were slim.

Marcus gave him his card on which he had written his home phone and cell phone numbers. "If you think of any information about Dr. Lieber, or remember anything that might be connected to this crime, please call me right away. Do we understand each other?"

"Of course. Thanks. I appreciate this. If I can be of help please call me."

"We'll be in touch."

Tomas nodded and left by the back door, taking care not to touch the door handle or screen where the investigators might find fingerprints of the last person to see Dr. Lieber alive.

* * *

Bonnie had gone straight to Hank Andrews' hospital room after driving fast from Dr. Lieber's office. If Hank had been awake when she got there, she would have confessed to it all. But he was asleep and so she merely slipped his Smith & Wesson under his pillow, gently patted his cheek and quietly left the hospital room.

She had no idea where to go. She couldn't quite get things straight in her head. She knew that her father had died. She knew that she wanted to go home; she wanted her mother. She wanted to hold her son and kiss his chubby little cheeks good night. But she was afraid. She just couldn't go home yet. What if her father's body was still there in the hogan? Bonnie began to shake, and to cry helplessly. Maybe if she drove around Hidden City she would be able to breathe right, and to think right.

She drove until she had almost no gas in the car, around and around the same six blocks, past the Dairy Queen and down Main to the library building. She remembered when she was in high school this is what she and her friends did on almost every Saturday night. It was comforting but where were her friends, they should be here, laughing and fixing each other's hair, worrying about the pound they had gained after eating all those french fries the night before.

The "low fuel" light flickered on. She noticed it and looked at the gauge: a hair from empty. Where was that Shell station? Just a block away, she remembered. She drove in the right direction, but remembered with an embarrassing jolt that the Shell station had been gone for years, torn down to be replaced by the Quikmart: part gas station, part grocery store. She pulled into the parking area. The pumps were all busy, so she thought that she would just park the car, around the back.

Bonnie was so tired that she coasted right into the gravel area and ran across the patch of grass and rocked slowly and gently into the shrub fence that served as landscaping for the Quikmart. The Cavalier engine stalled and sputtered and died. Not a soul saw her, except for the young man coming out of the Quikmart with a full plastic bag hanging from his hand.

Possum saw Bonnie, saw her head bounce forward when the car stopped against the bushes. Bonnie's head stayed pushed against the steering wheel.

Possum stopped to tie a knot in the top of his plastic bag. He didn't want anyone, not even Bonnie, see what was in the bag. He went to the car window and rapped with his closed knuckles on the glass. Bonnie didn't move very much but he thought she moved a little. He didn't think that she could be dead-her head had not knocked hard on the steering wheel, just a little bump was all.

He knocked harder and when she didn't move, he tried to

open the door. It was locked. He wanted to see her face to make sure that it was not bleeding. He walked around the car and tried the passenger side door. It opened. Setting his bag on the seat he leaned in and looked at Bonnie. Her eyes were closed. Tentatively Possum poked Bonnie on her right shoulder. She made a sound-something like nuuhh--and pulled away. Relieved, Possum moved backward and took hold of his plastic bag, to pull it out of the car. The bag bumped on the floor and caught Bonnie's purse that had been resting on the floor mat. In the dark Possum could not see what he was dragging. The open purse tipped, spilling its contents on the gravel. Possum jumped back. What hit the ground first was the biggest gun that Possum had ever seen.

Possum froze and looked around. No one was in sight. What should he do? He couldn't just leave the gun and the purse and all that stuff that Bonnie had in her purse spilled out on the ground. Carefully he scooped Bonnie's wallet and hairbrush and lipstick back into the leather bag --everything but the gun. He was worried about the gun. Bonnie was Sprite's friend, he had seen them talking and laughing when he poured coffee for them at the Coop. She might get into trouble with the police if anyone found the gun. He would get into trouble with the police if he took it with him. He thought hard.

Possum took another look at Bonnie's tired face. She was snoring lightly and Possum didn't want to try to wake her up again. He couldn't let Sprite's friend get into trouble. Possum put her purse back in the car on the passenger floorboard, and locked the door. Looking around again in the dark parking lot, he cautiously picked up the gun and took it into the bushes at the nose of the car. He hung it on a broken branch of the biggest cypress in the clump, deep in the fork. No one would find it there unless he showed them where to look.

Possum picked up his bag and headed back to the street, back into the spot of bright light that shone from the row of gas pumps. He began to walk in the general direction of Gigi's house. Maybe he would tell her what had happened and about the gun. He could even bring her back here if she didn't believe him.

Possum's excitement grew with every step he took that brought him closer to Gigi. He began to swing the heavy bag that was filled with the bottles of hydrogen peroxide that Gigi told him to buy. He didn't know how many bottles it would take to make him have blonde hair, hair as blonde as Gigi's own long soft hair. So he had bought all that they had at the Quikmart, six bottles in all. If there had been more on the shelf he would have bought them too. There is no such thing as too much for a man in love.

Chapter 26

Shortly after dawn, the first shift manager of the Quikmart noticed the blue Cavalier had overshot the edge of the parking lot and settled in the shrubbery. She assumed that the driver, whose face was turned away from the passenger door window, had too much to drink the night before but managed to get off the street before she passed out. It wasn't the first time a drunk had turned up in the parking lot.

The manager called the city police who showed up a half hour later to roust Bonnie.

"Come on now, get up, step out of the car," the officer said. He had to speak loudly because the windows were shut and the doors were locked. His voice boomed even louder in the thin air of morning. An occasional car drove by on the street but it was still early, too early for the brief burst of traffic as people hurried to work.

Bonnie remained slumped at the wheel. The officer began to rap on the side passenger window until Bonnie stirred. A thin line of saliva had crusted on her lower lip. She opened one eye and saw the officer looking at her through the glass. As quickly as she could she straightened up and wiped her mouth with the knuckle of her left hand.

"Open the door!" the officer commanded.

Frightened, Bonnie did as she was told. She felt hung over, and didn't know how she had landed in the bushes in her car.

Bonnie got out of the car stiffly. She saw the stare of the day manager of the Quikmart and remembered that she had driven into the parking lot to buy gas.

The officer recognized Bonnie but asked for her

identification anyway. She reached into the car for her purse and began digging around in it to find her wallet. There was something different…the gun. It was in her purse last night, she knew that. And now it was gone.

The officer scrutinized the driver's license and then asked for the registration and insurance card for the vehicle. So far he had not detected any smell of alcohol on Bonnie and there were no open bottles of liquor in the car. He couldn't think of anything here that would warrant even a traffic ticket. Bonnie was still standing by the car.

"Why were you sleeping in the parking lot?" the officer asked.

"I—I don't know." Bonnie replied.

"Are you sick? It looked like you had passed out. Like you had been drinking," the officer added. He knew that sometimes people passed out from diabetes, and had to have medicine quickly.

"No," said Bonnie. "I guess I just stayed up too long. I should go home. My mother will be worrying about me."

"Go on then. Get some sleep at home."

Bonnie nodded her head and climbed back into the driver's seat.

* * *

Gigi had Possum where she wanted him: in the beauty chair. Well, okay, it was her parents' upholstered dining room chair pulled into the kitchen, but she had turned the kitchen into something that resembled a beauty salon. Her parents were out of town; they said they thought Gigi was old enough to stay at home for a couple of days. Gigi nearly screamed with excitement, she had wanted to be trusted and to have some privacy, a rare treat in this small house.

As soon as the parents were out of the driveway Gigi began to makeover the kitchen. She was going to start with Possum and if he turned out nice then she would casually ask a couple of her friends if they would like to come to her salon for a treatment. Gigi had bought magazines and borrowed some of her father's good white shirts to use as spa robes. The shirts, she thought, were a nice business touch. Someday when she had her own salon she would have some special robes made to look like men's white business shirts, with her name embroidered in red or maybe silver handwriting on the breast: GIGI.

The girls who would work in her shop would wear white shirts and black pants; that would be the uniform. And she would make sure that they did each other's hair each day before serving any customers. If there was one thing that she could not stand it was going into a salon and having your hair cut by someone whose own hair was just awful. It wasn't good for business, not at all.

Gigi took a big mirror off the wall in the upstairs hallway and carried it downstairs to set up against the wall where she was creating her station. She washed all the dishes --wouldn't her mom be surprised by that – and arranged a stack of clean towels on the scrubbed counter. Everything had to be spic and span.

Gigi worked hard into the evening. She wasn't at all tired. Creating a facial center near the kitchen sink with a full sterling tray of all the creams and lotions and cleansers that she could find in her mother's bathroom. She set about sterilizing the instruments: tweezers and toenail clippers and metal combs and eyelash curlers. She thought about microwaving them but remembered at the last moment that you weren't supposed to put anything made of metal into the microwave. Thank God I remembered, I might have died! Gigi imagined.

She was nearly ready for Possum. She looked around and decided that she needed a reception area. She pulled a small table in the hallway out into the tiny entryway of the kitchen. Gigi arranged a tiny bouquet of sage and goldenrod that grew out by the trash cans behind the garage and placed it by a pad of paper and a handheld calculator, next to her father's Cross pen that he kept in its original box in his dresser drawer. She sat down and began to flip through the magazines.

Gigi looked at the ads for New York City's fine spas. She studied every corner and then squinted at her own set up. She could see that she needed more little lights around the makeup mirror to make the nice glow that she saw in the pictures. Then she noticed something that she had forgotten in her shop: in most of the magazine pictures, the ladies were holding a sparkling glass of something. Wine, Gigi decided. The beautiful ladies with their clean shaven long legs sat back in the chairs with towels wrapped around their heads, their long fingers wrapped around glasses of wine.

I can do that, Gigi thought. Mom and Dad have some wine in the basement. I'll just use a little for my customers. They won't mind.

By the time Possum arrived with his bag of peroxide, Gigi was all set.

* * *

Possum was knocked out, to say the least, when he saw Gigi. She had pulled her hair up into a long ponytail and lined her blue eyes with bluer eyeliner. Layer after layer of mascara on her lashes and bubble-gum pink lipstick made her look so sexy that Possum nearly dropped his shopping bag. The kitchen was warm and shining with light. Gigi's perfume rose to his nostrils and he drank the whole scene in where he would keep it always. She had done this for him, just for him. Was it possible that she liked him in the way that he liked her?

But Gigi was all business. She greeted him and wrote his name down on the pad of paper that she had on the table that blocked most of the kitchen doorway. She asked if she could take his coat. Possum looked down at his black sweatshirt, it wasn't a coat but it was something like a coat, and it was all he ever wore over his AC/DC tee shirts from fall until the first warm days of spring. But if Gigi wanted it, she could have it. He pulled off the sweatshirt and solemnly handed it to her.

"Did you get the peroxide, like I asked you to?" she whispered.

Possum didn't know why she was whispering—he thought and hoped that they were all alone in the house --but he handed her the heavy bag and whispered back, here it is.

She laughed when she saw the half dozen large bottles of peroxide. "This is a lot," she said.

"Well, what if the first bottle doesn't work?" Possum asked.

Gigi gave him a look that told him he didn't know the first thing about going blonde. She laughed again. Possum blushed with shame.

She saw his stricken face and reached out to pat his cheek. "It's okay," she said. "I'm the one who is supposed to know what to do here."

Possum felt better knowing that she wasn't mad at him.

"Come into my shop," she said. "First we'll wash your hair, then I'm going to cut you. Then I'll mix up the dye and foil some of your tips. I won't do anything too dramatic the first time. If you want more highlights we can always do that next time."

Possum caught on the words next time and relaxed. It was almost like she was his girlfriend already.

Gigi only spilled a little bit of peroxide on her dad's shirt, but she didn't think that he would mind. He had at least two other white shirts and might not even miss this one. It wasn't as easy cutting Possum's long hair as she thought it would be—it just wouldn't come out even, and she had to keep cutting to try to straighten it out. "These scissors are no good!" she told Possum. Her cheeks had reddened with the effort of the project, but her eyes were still sparkling with her youth and the excitement of making over Possum. "Wait until they see you at the Coop!" she assured him. "The girls won't be able to leave you alone."

Possum couldn't imagine what girls she might be thinking of; he only cared what she thought. He only hoped she wouldn't be able to leave him alone.

Finally the little pieces of foil were wrapped and folded here and there on the top and sides of his head. She set the egg timer for twenty minutes. Suddenly she didn't know what to do. "Would you like a magazine?" she asked. "Or how about a glass of wine?"

Possum was in heaven. He didn't care about a magazine, and he was afraid of the wine, but he said yes anyway. It was the night of his life. He took the glass of wine and drank it down like water. He didn't want her to think he had never had wine before but the fact was he hadn't. But this wine--it was sweet and red and left a stain on his mouth like he had eaten a box of strawberries.

Gigi had never drunk wine either and just did what Possum did, drinking it down like cherry coke. "Wow," Possum said, "That tasted good."

"Everyone in New York gets a glass of wine when they go to the salon, said Gigi.

"But we're not in New York," Possum said. "We're in Arizona."

Gigi tossed her ponytail, "Well we can pretend, can't we?"

Possum thought that was the funniest thing he had ever heard.

He was so impressed with her and what she knew about the big city, that he wanted to brag to her, too.

"I held a real gun before I came over here," he said. The wine was making him feel funny, and warm.

"What for?" Gigi asked. She was dizzy all of a sudden, but it felt good.

"I guess I was saving someone," Possum decided to say.

Gigi pushed him on the shoulder. "That's a lie. You didn't save anyone, did you, really?"

Possum became more sure in the telling. "I did. And I hid the gun in a tree."

Gigi was having a hard time thinking. She poured more wine into the tumblers that she had set before Possum and herself. The way Possum's head was feeling he wasn't sure he should drink more, but he couldn't let her down. Watching each other, they drank another big glass each.

The egg timer buzzer went off. "I guess you're done!" Gigi declared. She tried to stand up but her knees were wobbly. "Just tip your head this way," she said. Possum obliged and Gigi pulled off one of the foils and looked at his hair. "It doesn't look quite done," she said. "I think we should leave it on longer, maybe another twenty minutes."

"Okay," Possum slurred.

"Tell me who you saved." She still didn't quite believe him yet.

"It was one of Sprite's friends. They come to the Coop sometimes. She has a baby named Clay. I think her name is Bonnie."

Gigi gasped, "Oh my God, everyone is looking for her. Did you see her? Where was she?"

Possum told the story, only exaggerating slightly about the gun, saying that he thought maybe she was trying to kill herself in the car, but he had found her in time. He hid the gun so that she wouldn't get into trouble, and she just kind of went to sleep."

"Oh my God, Possum, we have to do something. Maybe she was taking sleeping pills or something too. What should we do?"

"Well I don't think we should do anything tonight. Or else I might be in trouble too." Possum was getting scared now, and the wine wasn't making him feel too well. He wasn't worried about the woman in the car or the gun until now, and --the wine was coming up. Possum breathed in the stench of the peroxide and the fumes of wine and he couldn't control the nausea. Gigi tried to get him to the bathroom in the hallway but she wasn't feeling too well herself. As they walked down the hall, bumping into each other and into the walls, she began to wretch. In the tiny bathroom he took the toilet, and she took the bathtub. It was not a pretty salon sight.

A half hour later, Possum lay with his still foiled cropped head in Gigi's soiled lap. Gigi's dad's shirts lay heaped on the floor, ripe with vomited wine stains. I'm going to have to wash those tomorrow, thought Gigi. Her Dad would not be happy if he saw his shirts.

* * *

When Bonnie returned to her mother's house, everyone was relieved to see her. Clara and her sisters hugged her and Clay held up his chubby arms to be picked up. Bonnie had virtually no memory of the past two days. It was like trying to remember the details of a dream, when she could almost remember what had happened, but the harder she tried the more any actual memory slipped away from her. The last thing she really remembered was taking her father's gun from his bedroom. It was in her purse, she knew that. But now the gun had disappeared as surely as her ability to remember the past.

Chapter 27

Dan Weatherford was pulled up in his usual chair beside Hank's bed as Hank groaned and slept and occasionally barked out an order to his deputy. His mood was not improving as the days went by and his worn body refused to heal like a younger man.

Cal Kingman had come to visit and sat in a straight back metal and plastic chair near the room's picture window. He twirled his cowboy hat between his hands and tried to talk to Hank. Dan and Cal had come to visit Hank after attending Dr. Lieber's funeral. They would have described it to Hank, who always attended the funeral of anyone that he knew even casually, to pay his respect, he always said. The public expected it. It was the kind of thing they remembered in the voting booth.

Hank stirred and opened his eyes and saw Dan and Cal sitting in his room. His mouth was so dry that his tongue stuck for a moment to the roof of his mouth. "Give me that glass of water," he demanded to Dan. Dan obligingly held the plastic cup so that Hank could take a couple of sucks on the striped straw.

"Did you boys get everything worked out?" Hank drawled.

Dan coughed nervously and crossed his legs. "I'm going to close the door, Hank."

Cal Kingman stood up and moved closer to Hank's bedside, carefully stepping around the cords and controls that lay tangled on the tile floor.

"We got it worked out, Hank, just fine. I want to thank you for turning me over to Dan; he's a good man. You know I wouldn't ask either one of you any favors unless I just have to. But every now and then a man needs his friends. You've been a good friend, Hank. I could not have stayed in business long without you helping me along."

Dan said nothing and kept his eyes fixed on the monitor that hung off the wall near Hank's bed. He saw the blood pressure numbers and the heart rate increase a little with Hank's efforts to talk.

Cal began to reminisce. "Sheriff do you remember that time we were in Washington and we took the congressman out to that place --I think it was across the bridge, over in Virginia. His boys tried to settle us down some; we were getting so loud and cutting up with the waitress? Do you remember that?"

Hank's eyes had closed again but a wry smile crossed his face. "I sure remember that it cost us a bucket of money. And that was just for the dinner..."

Dan watched the numbers grow on the electronic display. This was his opening.

"I'm sorry that I missed that, Hank. How much did it set you back?"

"I think it was $2,500. Pretty big money back then, but I guess now that would be chump change."

Dan gave a low long whistle. Cal looked at him, his eyes narrowing a little.

He and Dan had never talked any exact numbers. "Does that surprise you, Dan?" he asked carefully.

Dan looked at Cal levelly and said, "Heck no."

Hank was drifting off on the morphine. "Atta boy, Dan. Just remember it is a war out there. Good against evil you know, and we're in the good army, trying to protect business, and jobs, and paychecks. The government guys at the EPA-well I guess they are just trying to protect their paychecks too with their rules and permits and whatever bullshit they come up with this week. You just stick with your friends and do your job and you'll be fine. I'm tired now, boys, so if one of you will just help me turn this pillow over."

Dan got up and slipped his arm under Hank's damp head. With his other hand he reached under the pillow. His hand brushed something hard, his hand closed on the familiar shape of... a gun?

Dan pulled the gun out and Cal Kingman stepped back. Dan knew it was Hank's Smith & Wesson, he had seen it hundreds of times in Hank's office and on his belt. The question was how did it get under Hank's pillow? Cal raised his eyebrows and started to say something, but saw that Hank was sound asleep now and simply joked to Dan, "The NRA tooth fairy was here, I guess."

Dan made sure that the safety was on and then stuck the gun in his own belt. He needed to take it back to the office and lock it up himself. He would ask Hank about it later--and then raise hell with whoever had brought it to him in the hospital.

* * *

Dan paid a visit to Sprite at her office. She was confined to bed or a recliner upon Tomas' and her obstetrician's orders. The cramping that Sprite had begun to have after Jim's healing sing had not abated: it had only gotten worse.

Sprite wasn't used to being off her feet and wasn't very happy about the confinement. But she knew that it was best for the baby, so she grumpily cooperated.

Dan had brought her a chicken sandwich, french fries and a Coke for lunch. She decided to give herself a break--usually she stuck to grilled chicken, salad and milk for the baby's sake.

Dan was using the only bare patch of wood visible on her desk as a place to set his paper plate of fried chicken. Dan had told Sprite about the hospital room visit with Cal Kingman.

"It doesn't sound good," Dan said. "That part about spending money in Washington..."

Sprite interrupted, "sounds a lot like bribery, or a payoff."

Dan studied his hands. "What do we do now?"

"I'm not exactly sure, but I think we need to talk with the State's Attorney—just as soon as I can get out of this chair."

There was a knock on the office door,

Dan got up and opened the door. Possum stood there, his hair a wreck of patchy white spots. Sprite waved him in.

"Good grief, Charlie (his real name was Charles)," Sprite

said, "What happened to you?"

"Gigi gave me a makeover," he explained. His cheeks flushed.

Dan laughed. Sprite shot him a warning look.

"Well, Charles. It certainly is different. How do you like it?"

"Uh—I'm not so sure."

"Don't worry, Charles. The good thing about new haircuts is that it can all grow back pretty soon if we don't like them. Everybody goes through that."

"Gigi said I should come and talk to you."

"About the hair?" Sprite asked.

"No."

"Then what?"

Possum looked at Dan Weatherford, then back at Sprite.

"Uh, maybe I could come back later," he said.

"Come on Possum. Dan is a friend. What's on your mind?"

"Gigi said everybody at the Coop was looking for your friend, the one who has the little boy."

"Yes."

"I found her. She was in a car behind the Quikmart." Possum was watching their faces, trying to figure out if Bonnie was in trouble or what.

"That's great, Possum. You were right to come and tell us. We were worried about her."

Possum liked feeling that he had helped Sprite in something important. It was just like before, when he was the one who helped Tomas when he was in trouble with the police. He got to go to court to tell what had really happened. Maybe he would get to do that again. Gigi would like that.

"I found a gun."

Dan looked up quickly. "Where did you find a gun, son?"

"Bonnie had it in the car. She was asleep and I was afraid she was going to get into trouble, having that gun in the car where anybody could see it. I took it out, and I hid it. I wasn't going to hurt anybody," he added.

"What did you do with the gun, Charles? Asked Sprite gently. "It's important."

Possum said "It's in a tree, behind the Quikmart."

Dan said, "Would you like to ride in my car out to the Quikmart, and show me?"

"I'll have to ask Nick if I can go."

"Why don't I go with you to ask Nick?"

Possum looked relieved. Then a grin crossed his face as he realized that Gigi was working that day too and she would see him with the Deputy. Everyone would see how important he was.

"Okay." Possum said, grinning.

Dan Weatherford and Possum drove to the Quikmart in Dan's patrol car. Possum made sure that Gigi saw him get into the front seat; he gave her a thumbs up sign before he closed the passenger door. Gigi was impressed.

On the way to the Quikmart Dan asked Possum a lot of questions about what had happened the night he found Bonnie in her car. Dan was beginning to fear that Bonnie had something to do with Dr. Lieber's murder: he knew that she blamed him for her father's death, and that she was missing for more than a day on the day the doctor was murdered. And now, Possum talked about a gun that had been in her car.

The Quikmart was doing a brisk business that day. Dan saw the day manager look up and watch him before he drove slowly behind the building to the parking lot. Possum pointed out where Bonnie's car had been parked. Dan saw where the tire treads had mashed down the grass in parallel lines right up to the stand of small trees and shrubs.

Possum wanted to go get the gun for Dan, but Dan stopped him, saying that there might be fingerprints on it that he needed to see. Dan had Possum point out where the gun was, and then he gingerly lifted it off the stub of cypress branch with a pencil. He put it into a plastic bag that he marked with a piece of tape and some notes, then locked it in the trunk of his car.

Dan called Marcus Steamer on his direct line. Marcus picked up, "Steamer here."

"Hi, Marcus, it's Dan. Dan Weatherford. I'm calling to let you know that I have a gun in my possession that I would like for you to have checked out. It might be the one you are looking for in the Lieber case."

Possum could only hear one side of the conversation, but he was excited. The police were looking for a gun, and he had found one. He was still afraid for Bonnie and hoped that she wouldn't get into any trouble, but if he could help the police again…he ran his hand over the dry stubble of his hair. It looked and felt like a Navajo cornfield after the dried corn was cut in the fall. Still, she had done it, her hands on his head. Maybe she would go out with him if his name or even his picture got into the Pueblo Weekly News. He hoped they would let him hold the gun.

Dan talked on the phone a little longer and Possum heard him say, "I'll drive on up to Bonnie's and see if I can talk to her about this. I'm taking Possum with me to make the positive I.D."

Possum settled back in the squad car and closed his eyes so that he could hear better. "I'll call you again in a couple of hours," Dan said. If you want to pick up the gun for ballistics testing, maybe you could meet me at Bonnie's after I have a chance to talk with her."

Possum looked at Dan as he put on his brown, wide-brimmed deputy hat.

A hat like that could hide a lot of mistakes.

* * *

Spirit found it difficult to stay awake lately. She ate, and she slept and she tried to read, but it was hard to concentrate when a little leg or heel was suddenly pushing on your ribcage, or another part that wasn't designed to stretch. She felt huge and inflexible and about as unattractive as a woman could feel. The bulky cast caused her arm to itch like mad. She was too hot and then too cold, and always on the verge of tears.

Tomas was more concerned with her medical issues than with her moods. He understood well enough the hormonal roller coaster that's pregnancy and tried his best to distract her and to keep her company during the final weeks. He bought her

magazines—as many as he could from the grocery store rack—
and talked with her about color choices for the nursery in the
new house, anything to keep her mind off the discomfort of her
body.

Tomas and Spirit were at home in the trailer when Dan
Weatherford called from Bonnie's house. Tomas answered and
Dan spoke calmly but with an urgency that Tomas was not used
to in Dan's voice.

"Could you come up to Bonnie and Clara's house, Tomas?"

Tomas really didn't want to, and he didn't want to leave
Spirit alone tonight.

"What's going on, Dan?"

"Something's wrong with Bonnie. She won't talk to anyone
here and has been holed up in that hogan that they built for Jim's
healing. Clara said that she is not eating and she doesn't think
she is sleeping either."

Tomas sighed. He covered the phone mouthpiece and said
to Spirit, "It sounds like Bonnie is in real trouble. Dan wants me
to go have a look at her. Would you be all right here while I'm
gone?"

"Probably, but if Bonnie is in bad condition I might be able
to talk with her better than you can. I think that she trusts me.
You know, woman to woman."

Tomas knew she was right but was still reluctant to let her
go. The roads in that area weren't well maintained and if they
were to hit an unexpected pothole Tomas was afraid that the
jarring could cause more problems for Spirit and the baby.

Spirit insisted. "I'll be fine," she said. "Bonnie needs our
help."

* * *

Bonnie lay wrapped in a fleece on one of the woven rugs on
the floor of the hogan. She was dimly aware of Sprite and Tomas
leaning over her, and pulled the fleece tighter around her. Her
eyes were closed. Sprite saw the deep burgundy color that
encircled her eyes. It was startling against her ashen complexion.

"Bonnie?" Sprite called softly.

Bonnie clenched her eyes tighter.

"Honey, let us help you."

"No one can help me," Bonnie said.

"I can help you," Tomas said. "But we need to take you to the hospital. You need medicine."

"My mother can give me medicine."

Tomas nodded his head. "Your mother has good medicine. But you need something special. I can get you some medicine that will help you a lot."

Bonnie opened her tortured eyes and looked at Tomas. "I bet that's what that doctor told my father."

Tomas held one of her hands. Sprite held the other and said to Bonnie, "Tomas won't hurt you, Bonnie. I'll make sure. But we need to take you to the hospital. Will you let me help you?"

Bonnie saw Dan Weatherford as he ducked into the hogan. "Could I talk with him first?"

Tomas nodded to Spirit and then looked to Dan and motioned for him to join them near Bonnie.

Dan stepped nearer. It was close in the hogan and he had to drop down on his knees to join Tomas and Sprite.

"Let us help you, Bonnie," Dan said gently. He had never seen anyone in Bonnie's condition. She now seemed to be a small child, a forlorn little girl. Her voice when it came was as thin as a five year old's.

"I think I might have killed someone, Dan." Bonnie said.

Sprite's instinct to protect Bonnie kicked in. "Bonnie, don't say anything right now. Let's just get you to the hospital."

Dan was torn: If Bonnie had killed Dr. Lieber, if she was now confessing to a murder, then he was duty-bound to take action: he would have to arrest her. There was the gun, there was the motive, and no one could account for Bonnie's whereabouts on the day Dr. Lieber was shot. But was she lucid? He needed to be sure before he asked her any questions. A wrong step here, any questioning of her as a suspect when an ordinary person should be able to see that her mental state was seriously compromised, could provide a strong argument for a faulty arrest that could queer the whole case.

Sprite was looking at Dan to see what he would do next when a pain shot through her pelvis that nearly made her fall to the hard clay ground. She gasped and reached for Tomas. He released Bonnie's hand and moved quickly to Spirit's side. Her face had gone nearly as pale as Bonnie's. Gently Tomas eased her to the ground and said to Dan, "Call for an ambulance. For both of them."

Chapter 28

Sprite woke up in the Flagstaff surgical center with an IV in her right arm. She had almost no feeling below her waist and both of her feet and lower legs were encased in some kind of vinyl coverings that periodically pressed on her and then released. She knew this from watching the motion and from hearing the sounds. Sprite was trying to remember what had happened, but the last thing she recalled with any clarity was being lifted on a stretcher into an ambulance with Tomas beside her, anxiously talking with the EMT as they all endured a rocky, high-speed trip to the Flagstaff hospital.

She felt her belly and found it swaddled in bandages and a wide elastic band. She knew that the baby was gone.

Tomas was sprawled in a recliner chair near the foot of the bed. When he heard Sprite moving around in the bed he became fully awake; and rocked forward to put the recliner into an upright position. Sprite smiled wanly at him; he needed a shave.

"It's so good to see you awake," he said.

"What happened to me?" Sprite asked.

"Among other things, you had a baby," he began. Tomas suddenly remembered his first look at their daughter in the middle of the night. She was coated with the sticky birth fluids, but she was perfect. He thought that he would hold that vision in his heart forever.

"And?" Sprite said. Her eyes were filling with tears.

"We have a girl," said Tomas. He went to Spirit's bedside, lowered the guardrail and carefully positioned the IV line. He sat down on the edge of the bed and took her fingertips that showed from the edge of her cast. "She is perfect in every way."

The tears overflowed Spirit's eyes. She wanted to see her, right now.

"Where is she?" Spirit knew that they would name her soon, but there was time for that. "I want to see her and hold her."

Tomas reached for the call button dangling from the bed rail. "So do I," he said. "But there is something else I need to tell you."

Spirit knew from his tone and hesitation that the news would not be happy.

"Not yet," she begged. "Just let me see the baby first. Everything else can wait."

Tomas leaned in close to kiss the tears on her face. "Okay, honey. This is your day. Just tell me when you feel like talking."

A nurse opened the door and wheeled in an incubator. Spirit glimpsed a soft white blanket and a miniature pink face, the eyes no more than fine lines, as if drawn on the tender skin. Her tears began again but she tried to hoist herself higher upon on the bed. She felt a sharp pull from beneath the bandage on her abdomen, and had to stop herself. Tomas put his arm underneath her shoulders and helped her to sit up, while the nurse adjusted the bed frame. Then she turned and lifted the bundle out of the heated incubator and handed the baby to Spirit.

Tomas and Spirit looked at their daughter in fascination and awe. It was as if they had never seen a newborn baby before. The baby had arrived prematurely but seemed to be perfectly healthy. Spirit was especially intrigued by the baby's long fingers, like tiny translucent starfish that curled into tight fists. She imagined that the baby had looked just like this inside her, with its legs folded close and tucked up as if ready to cannonball into the world.

Tomas recalled his days in medical school when he regarded babies and new mothers with a clinician's detachment, now swallowed his own joyful tears. The little girl was the image of Spirit. It was what he had hoped for during the long months of pregnancy. The delicacy of her skull and the slant of her nose--it was all Spirit. Right down to the full head of dark brown hair.

His daughter was all that he wished for, and she would be the only child they would ever have of their own blood. Tomas carried this knowledge that in the long dark night, the obstetrical team had to make a weighty decision. The surgeon in charge consulted with Tomas before beginning the emergency C-section, but they both knew that there was no real room for debate. To safely deliver the little girl and preserve Spirit's life, the uterus itself, with the threatening tumor now grown to the inner wall like a house guest that had stayed on too long, would have to be removed. Spirit would carry no more children, but she would live. It was too soon to tell if the tumor was malignant or benign, although Tomas' gut feeling was that it was benign. Easy now, one step at a time, he told himself. The lab specimens would be given priority but it would still be hours before they would have all of the results.

He wanted to name her, but he knew that Spirit would also have her preferences. The naming was important and would not be done lightly. It should reflect her own special qualities, not just now but for her entire life. So it was better not to rush. He would meditate and pray on this just as his ancestors had done in their ceremonies.

What's this? Tomas thought. Prayer ceremonies and meditations? I'm a modern man. A scientist. We don't look to spirits for guidance. We use logic and laws of physics, microscopes and ... He stopped himself. Something was different. Something no longer fit.

Spirit handed Tomas the baby. She opened her eyes, blinking against the light that shone from the hospital light fixture. Tomas briefly wondered what it was like for her at this moment, to go from the watery darkness of the womb to air and light. It was a new beginning for the child, and the child was a new beginning for Tomas and Spirit. They could never truly leave each other again, no matter the circumstances, no matter their differences. They were united in this creation they called "daughter." There was no logic and no science to explain Tomas' feeling of devotion and the depth of his desire to protect the child, and to protect Spirit. He was a changed man.

* * *

As the new soul of Spirit and Tomas' baby was entering the world, another's light was fading. Across the desert in a Hidden City hospital room, Sheriff Hank Andrews was losing his battle with the infection that had entered his bloodstream even after he had survived the long and complicated open heart surgery that was meant to give him more time.

Dan Weatherford knew the moment he walked into Hank's room that something had changed. There was a smell to the room that was cloying, both sweet and putrid at the same time. The nurses who attended to Hank wore face masks, and required Dan to do the same.

Dan asked the nurse assigned to Hank to give him her off-the-record opinion of the outlook. "I can tell you what I think, but at this point it's in God's hands," she said.

Dan decided to stay for longer than he had initially planned. The nurse brought him a fresh cup of coffee and sat down with him for a moment.

"I don't like the looks of this," she said, reading his chart. "And I don't like the looks of him even more." She checked the undersides of his toes and noticed the black specks that grew increasingly larger. The blood was pooling; circulation was failing. The fingertips were similarly discolored. "Dan, I think that if there is anything you want to say to Hank Andrews, this would be the time. I'll leave you alone."

She closed the door and Dan stood by the bed awkwardly. Hank was coming to consciousness and there was something Dan needed to know. He patted Hank's arm and called his name.

Hank opened his eyes. Dan gave him a sip of water from the plastic cup that the nurse had refilled with ice chips." Hank's lips were dehydrated but he was able to speak.

"Dan," he said. "Nice to see you."

Dan swallowed hard. "Boss," he began.

He didn't know what to say next.

Sheriff Andrews' face was burnished with fever and damp

with perspiration. His labored breathing caused his upper chest to rise and fall rapidly. "Are you keeping the bad guys in line out there?" he asked.

"I'm doing my best, sir."

"I was glad to see Cal Kingman the other day," said Hank. "It has been a while since we ran around together. We had us some good times though."

Dan was relieved that Hank had provided him a way to open up the subject that had been worrying him. "I was wondering about those times, sir."

Hank closed his eyes and swallowed hard. "I figured you would, son."

Don't call me son, please don't call me son, thought Dan. He was so used to looking up to Hank Andrews as both mentor and friend and something like a father that he couldn't bear to lose Hank and to know that he was not all that Dan had believed for all these years.

"Hank," Dan said. "There is something I really have to know."

Hank seemed to be going back to sleep; his lips sent out small, regular explosions of air in puffs.

"Dan," said the Sheriff, "let me make this easier for you. If you are wondering if Cal Kingman and I broke the law, the answer is, not in the beginning. Like most things in life, it was not a clear-cut situation twenty or thirty years ago. Everything is different now."

"I can't believe you would get involved..." Dan said quietly.

"There were a lot of us who felt we were in the right. That the government was trying to go too far and it was hurting good people who were just trying to do business. To make a living for their families and give jobs to people who were desperate to work and to feed their families. I was just in a position to help a little."

Dan said, "I don't believe I'll be taking your position, Sheriff." He felt a band of pain tighten around his own chest.

Sheriff Andrews nodded almost imperceptibly.

Dan turned and walked tiredly out of the room. He didn't look back as he made his way through the corridors and out to the parking lot. In the privacy of his squad car, hot tears came and he had no choice but to let them flow. Then he blew his nose with his handkerchief and twisted the key in the ignition. The engine jumped to life. Dan knew that he had talked with Hank Andrews for the last time.

By noon the next day, the county's long term sheriff was dead. Dan Weatherford remained the acting Sheriff and would have to decide whether to seek to run for election. He sat for a long time at the Coop, nursing a cup of coffee and avoiding conversation with everyone. He looked older: a combination of too little sleep and too much on his mind. Dan should have gone home and gotten some sleep, but he feared that his wife would only start in on him for staying out all night again. No, there was no rest there. He found himself slumped on Hank's worn couch, where he had occasionally taken an afternoon rest. It was the closest he could get to feeling at home anywhere. Pulling his hat over his face, he slept.

* * *

Clara Hammer made the trip from her home to Flagstaff in the passenger seat of her sister's pickup truck. The visiting hours for the Psychiatric Services floor were extremely limited: only one hour in the evening on Tuesday and Thursday during the week, and one hour on Sunday afternoon. When Clara protested the limited visiting hours, a nurse informed her that often the patient's main problem is a family member. Clara thought that she spoke the term like it was a dirty word. Clara fumed. The nurse further informed Clara that she would have to be on the approved visitor list to be able to visit at all.

Clara asked for the nurse's name. She might want to have a word with the woman's supervisor before this was done. The idea of treating her, Bonnie's own mother, like a meddling stranger added insult to Clara's pain.

To help soothe her daughter's nerves Clara had brewed

some tea made from the lemon balm that grew rampantly in her sister's border garden. Aunt Tess had brought bundles of the fragrant herb when she came for the healing ceremony. Clara and Tess both drank a cup of the tonic and then poured the rest into a glass lined thermos to take to Bonnie.

The nurse had asked Clara to bring Bonnie some of her clothes to wear at the hospital. Even though Bonnie wanted only to stay in bed, hiding under her wool blankets, the hospital required all the patients to come out of their rooms each day, and to stay in the day room --doing nothing but watching TV or reading the slim selection of magazines and novels that accumulated on bolted down bookshelves that lined one wall of the large, noisy room.

When Clara signed in on the Visitor's log, she had to leave her purse at the nurses' station. The tea was dumped down the sink and the thermos bottle was kept with Clara's purse--no glass was allowed on the ward, the nurse said briskly. The paper bag that contained Bonnie's clothes was dumped out by a nurse onto a card table and the clothing examined piece by piece. Clothes with buttons weren't allowed. Clothes with zippers weren't allowed. Clothes with drawstrings were certainly not allowed. When Clara asked why, the nurse looked at her like she was stupid and said "This is a psych floor. It's for their own protection."

Eventually Clara was permitted to enter the day room where she found Bonnie sitting near the nurses' station observation window. Bonnie looked at her without expression and didn't rise to greet her. Clara went to her and put both arms around her and just held on. Clara seemed to need a hug more than Bonnie did, and when she finally let go Clara had to turn her face to the television set until her own tears subsided.

Bonnie seemed extremely sleepy and didn't respond to Clara's attempt to make conversation. "Is the food okay here?" Clara asked.

Bonnie shrugged her shoulders.

"I brought you some clothes."

Bonnie frowned and said, very slowly and deliberately, "Those jeans that I had on..." She could not remember if it was yesterday, or the day before that, or even the day before that --a lot was missing from her memory.

Clara was confused. "Well, I couldn't bring you any jeans honey, only some of your running pants with the elastic waistband. So don't worry about it if they are stained, I'll wash them before you come back home."

Bonnie began to chew the corner of one fingernail. Clara noticed that most of her nails were chewed to the quick and were inflamed. Her eyes were those of a hunted animal.

Clara gave up on conversation after a while and simply took Bonnie's hand and held it in her own. Holding hands, they stared at the Wheel of Fortune that turned every night at 6:00. Clara studiously avoided looking at the other patients in the day room. My daughter, she thought, has nothing in common with them. I will take her home as soon as I can and get her well again. We will all get well again.

Chapter 29

Tomas was deep in thought over the name they would give their daughter as he made his way through the corridors of the hospital when it was time for him to go home.

When he reached the lobby he was surprised to see Clara Hammer. She looked older as her shoulders slumped and she walked on tired legs. Tomas caught up with her and touched her on the shoulder.

Clara reacted with a start; she had not heard his steps behind her. When she saw that it was Tomas, she did her best to smile.

"Hello, Clara,"

Clara greeted him and then asked about Sprite. "Are you a father yet?" she asked.

It was the first time anyone had said the word father in reference to him. "Yes," he said "We have a little girl. She is doing just fine. And Sprite?"

"Tired. She had an emergency C-Section. There were some complications, but she is a strong woman. I think that she'll be okay."

Ordinarily Clara would have inquired further about Sprite, but her mind was on Bonnie. Tomas sensed her distraction and fatigue. "How are you getting home?" he asked.

"My sister is waiting in the parking lot for me. She will drive me home, but then she has to go on to her own family."

"I'm going to be going your way. Would you like for me to drive you to your house?"

Clara thought this over as they walked. It would save her sister a lot of driving and she had been doing so much for Clara already during the past weeks.

"Let me talk with my sister. I think that might work out for the best, if you don't mind."

"I don't mind at all. How is Bonnie?"

Clara didn't know what to say. But Tomas was a doctor, maybe he could answer some of Clara's questions. It would be good to have his attention on the long ride home.

"My daughter seems like a different person. I'm afraid for her. And that hospital..."

Tomas held her arm like an escort as they neared the parking lot. "This is all so new, Clara. And so soon after Jim's death. It is going to take a long time to straighten out, I think."

Clara nodded.

Clara's sister was relieved to be able to go on home, and Clara was lucky to have help from Tomas. He could even get her some medicine if she needed it, although Clara believed far more in her herbal remedies.

During the ride home Clara asked Tomas many questions about his family. She knew that he was of Cherokee heritage and had come from the east to be with Sprite. Tomas soon found himself talking about his great grandfather, Jawotnehe, the talented shaman who used many herbs in his healing ceremonies. Clara shyly told Tomas of her own experiments with plants and told him about her healing garden that she was cultivating near the stream that formed the western boundary to their family property.

The problem, Clara said, was that many of the plants that she needed simply would not grow well in the alkaline soil of the desert. Herbs liked woods and rich black soil such as her grandmother had on the farm in eastern Oklahoma. The woody herbs required a lot of water, and water was scarce. She needed to learn more about the cactus and other desert plants, as well as the skills of the healers, to be able to help her family and neighbors. She felt her own strength and her connections to Father Sky and Mother Earth, but she still needed the tools to work with.

Tomas understood completely. He missed his own tools that

he had taken for granted in Atlanta: the hospital diagnostic machines such as the MRIs and the CT scans. The sophisticated laboratories, and the computers and robotics and most of all the other doctors. He had a chance at regaining some of those tools when he met Terry Lieber and now that resource was lost. His professional future was like a black box to him.

Clara looked at him shyly. "Tomas," she said, "You have the skills of a healer, and the best of both worlds. It seems that you have the spirit of your great-grandfather, the one you called Jawotnehe. And you also have the white man's medicine. You have used the white man's medicine for so long, but now it is hiding from you out here in the desert. Do you think you are now supposed to let your great-grandfather's healing ways grow stronger? Do you believe that you have more to learn of the old ways?"

Once again, Tomas' world seemed to tilt. It was true that he had gone far over to the white man's medicine. When he lost the coordination in his left hand and arm from the mild stroke that he had suffered, he had to stop his surgical practice. Then fate had cast him out into the desert without the benefit of clean white rooms and shining laboratories. What was happening here? Was there a message that he had been ignoring?

And now there was Clara. He stole a look at her profile and saw the grief for her daughter etched there. But he also saw the strong cheekbones, the kind and accepting eyes, the keen intelligence. She waited patiently for his reply.

Tomas found himself telling Clara what he had not yet told Sprite: that she would have no more children, the result of the damaged uterus. Clara looked at him with pity.

She was learning about loss and all of the masks that it wore in people's lives.

"Don't give up, Tomas."

"What do you mean? We will have no more children, it can't happen. All of the charms, prayers and dances in Arizona can't change that."

"Maybe so, maybe not. Something in my mind's eye sees

you with a son and a daughter."

Tomas raised an eyebrow and exchanged looks with the older woman. "I don't see how," he said.

"Neither do I, at the moment, but the feeling is strong. And I have come to trust my feelings."

Tomas wondered if she was just trying to make him feel better.

The Vanquish covered the miles between the hospital and Clara's home all too soon. Tomas felt at home with Clara, and she with him. He hoped that he would see her again. He was curious about her experiments with her healing garden and knew that he could learn much from her, and from her teachers. The immediate pressure to find a cure for Spirit was passed if the tumor was benign, as he suspected. It was crazy, but like Clara, his intuition that he was about to enter into a different world--his ancestors' world, was coming on strong.

Just before Tomas and Clara arrived at her house, Clara asked Tomas the question that she had wanted to ask for the entire time of the car ride.

"Tomas, what's wrong with Bonnie?"

Tomas pressed his lips together. He was no psychiatrist, but his experience in medicine pointed in the direction of a serious mental illness. He couldn't be sure, but the short time that he observed Bonnie indicated a psychotic break. But how could he explain that to Clara right now? She had suffered so much lately. If she understood the concept, she was at risk herself for slipping into a depression that might require hospitalization. And he didn't know for sure.

"The doctors will help to sort that out, Clara."

"I don't trust that hospital. They seem to like to push people around. So many rules. They wouldn't even let me give Bonnie the tea that I brought to her. It would have helped her, I know."

"I'm sure it would. It's just that the hospital has to take care of so many people that any one patient gets lost in the crowd. They have to make the rules for everyone. Try not to take it personally, Clara."

"I just want to bring her home and use my kind of medicine to help her get well."

He reached over and patted her hand. "I'm sure you will be able to do that. I'll help you out if you like, as much as I can."

Clara looked at him gratefully. "I'll help you out too."

When Tomas pulled the Vanquish into the driveway of Clara's home, a Sheriff's car was pulled up close to the house. Another police car was parked beside it, and all the lights were on in the house.

Tomas and Clara hurried into the house. Inside, another of Clara's sisters and her husband were sitting anxiously in the living room. Bonnie's son, Clay, played with a small metal pickup truck on the worn carpeting. From upstairs, they heard heavy footsteps.

Tomas and Clara looked at her sister. Before either of them could say a word, they heard hurried steps coming down the stairs and then saw the lean frame of Dan Weatherford duck into the living room.

He went to Clara and held her hands. "Where is Bonnie?" he asked.

"She's in the hospital," said Clara. The nurse said that she would probably be there for a while.

Another sheriff's deputy came into the room, carrying what looked like Bonnie's blue jeans in a sealed plastic bag. "What are you doing with Bonnie's jeans?" Clara asked.

Dan looked down at his feet. "We have to take them with us, Clara. They might have blood on them. I'm so sorry, Clara, but we're going to have to arrest Bonnie. We think that she shot Dr. Lieber."

Clara's knees buckled. If Tomas had not been nearby to catch her, she would have fallen to the floor.

* * *

By the end of the week Sheriff Hank Andrews was laid to rest with little public fanfare--just the way he wanted. Over the years Hank and Dan Weatherford had quite a few conversations about their wishes for final goodbyes. Hank was a firm believer in cremation. He told Hank that good workable dirt was too scarce in Arizona to be wasted on burying bodies; cremation was the only thing that made sense.

The only thing he asked, Dan remembered, was that he be dressed in full law enforcement dress uniform, including his gunbelt and his Smith & Wesson. That weapon had seen him through some rough times, and he wasn't about to go into the afterlife unarmed. It was an unusual request, according to the funeral director, but certainly not impossible to carry out. When the remains of Sheriff Hank were handed over to Acting Sheriff Dan Weatherford, the rectangular wooden box was particularly heavy. . Dan had not been given any instructions as to what to do with Hank's ashes. After some consideration, Dan placed the box on top of the gun rack. It seemed as good of a final resting place as any.

There would be a memorial service for the sheriff in a few weeks. The sheriff's list of friends and political acquaintances stretched back for decades and numbered in the hundreds. Other law enforcement agencies would want to attend, and to honor him with eulogies and an honor guard that would line the sidewalk and out into the street of the funeral home. There would a luncheon later where groups of men and women would eat chicken salad sandwiches and potato salad and drink too much coffee. People would slap Dan on the back as if everyone knew he would be the replacement for Sheriff Andrews but also knew it was too soon for a spoken "Congratulations."

As the days went by Dan grew more comfortable in the sheriff's shoes. There was a lot to deal with and he dealt with his private grief over the loss of his friend and boss by keeping busy; trying harder than usual to be the professional that he aspired to be.

He'd received a telephone message from Cal Kingman after Hank's death was announced in the newspaper. Kingman wanted to get together with Dan, maybe have some lunch. Dan didn't return the call. He was not yet ready to deal with Cal Kingman.

* * *

Marcus Steamer was as perplexed as he had ever been in his long career with the Navajo Tribal Police. He felt confident that they knew who killed Dr. Terry Lieber. They had it all --or almost all --and the evidence clearly pointed to Bonnie as the one who had pulled the trigger. There was only one problem. The gun that Bonnie had in her possession on the day that Dr. Lieber was shot was not the gun that had fired the bullets.

No matter how many times he tested the Smith & Wesson, it left the same "fingerprint" on the test bullets. The fingerprints on the bullets retrieved from the crime scene were as different as the unique fingerprints of two different people. There was no mistake. Bonnie's gun had not been the murder weapon.

When Marcus Steamer called Dan Weatherford to share that information, Dan couldn't believe it. As much as he liked Bonnie--and he liked her a lot--he had no doubt that she had gone to Dr. Lieber's clinic in her confused state of mind and killed him. It would be his job to make sure that Bonnie was brought to justice, and he was prepared to do his job. Now, the case had a hole in it that was big enough to walk through to freedom.

Sure, Bonnie had virtually confessed to him, and had a strong motive for the murder. But the problem with the ballistics unnerved Dan. Somewhere, there had been a mistake.

* * *

Ed was virtually finished with Tomas and Spirit's new home. He was finishing the doors and windows with several coats of polyurethane and getting ready to put the final touches-- the little things that made it his creation, when he heard the news that the baby had been born. She was early, but she was healthy. The baby and the mother would need a home very soon. Tomas joined Ed to help him with the installation of the window locks and door locks, and clean up. Tomas didn't want a speck of dust to show when he brought his family home.

As he sat on a saw horse in the family room, looking out at the golden light that infused the ravine with a fairy tale picture of late autumn, Tomas remembered his grandmother telling him the story of the Sun, how the sun was the beginning of everything new and good for the earth. Out of the darkness came the light and people were able to grow plants for food. The birth of his daughter was a new beginning for Tomas, and it was at that moment that he heard the call of her name: Luz, meaning "light." She would be the light of his life, along with Spirit. He could hardly wait to share his idea with his wife, and only hoped that she would like it as much as he did.

Luz Hotone. A perfect name for a perfect child. Tomas looked out the window again and spotted a small pine tree silhouetted against the blue sky at the opposite side of the ravine. It would be their Christmas tree.

Chapter 30

When Bonnie's gun didn't match up with the bullets that had been fired into Dr. Lieber, it was back to square one for Marcus Steamer. He sat before Dr. Terry Lieber's computer, staring at the beige box. He considered how the invention had changed the world, and wondered what was to come next as technology marched unstoppable, bringing more and more information, faster and easier, to the farthest corners of the world. Here, in his world, he was counting on the box to help him understand the murder of its owner, Dr. Lieber.

Dr. Lieber had been a careful researcher who made extensive notes both in the records of the patients, and also in his private journaling. He was a habitual email user, and frequented various chat rooms. Marcus knew you could learn a lot about a person by knowing where they visited in cyberspace. For Dr. Lieber, he concluded that he was obsessed with proving his theory that chelation therapy was the cure for just about everything--but especially for cancer. He seemed to live and breathe his work, almost like he had no other interests in his life.

Marcus tried several simple exercises to investigate Dr. Lieber's activities over the past ten years. First, he used the "Search" command to find each file that contained the term "chelation." Whether the term was used in a patient's file, a research note, or an e-mail, it showed up as a listing. Out of curiosity, Marcus began sorting the search results into different time frames, and created a year-by-year profile of the appearances of different phrases. The data showed a steady growth of the use of the term "chelation therapy" in all the sources of information: files, folders, links to websites, and e-mail messages.

Computers are great, thought Marcus. He began to read each listing, paying heightened attention to the patient records. His private belief was that Dr. Lieber had been shot by a disappointed patient, someone who was going to die anyway and had a bone to pick with Dr. Lieber. In his perusal of the records and personal journal entries Marcus looked for clues that Dr. Lieber had an enemy or two, and that he wrote something down that might be helpful.

Marcus Steamer was hindered in his research by his lack of medical knowledge. He was in over his head when it came to deciphering some of the notes in the personal journal. He needed a doctor to talk with about the information he had gleaned from the files.

Marcus had the telephone number of Tomas Hotone stapled to his file folder on the Lieber murder investigation. He had been reluctant to call Tomas until Tomas had been cleared of any suspicion himself--but that was not a real concern now. Marcus picked up the telephone and called Tomas. "I appreciate your offer to help on Dr. Lieber's case," Marcus said. "I could use a little help with the medical information that I'm finding on the computer."

Tomas was not about to pass up the chance to have a look into Dr. Lieber's notes. "Of course," he said into his cell phone. "I'll come up tonight if it will help. Right now I'm getting to know my new daughter."

Marcus smiled and expressed his congratulations to Tomas and asked about Sprite.

"She's learning how to be a mom," Tomas said. Sprite made a face as she heard him say this. She was trying for the third time that morning to persuade her baby to nurse, but the infant's mouth was so small that it wasn't going particularly well. The fathers have the easy part in all this, she thought.

When Tomas put down the cell phone Spirit asked him about the call. "I can't quite put my finger on it," Tomas said, "But something is bothering me about Dr. Lieber's research." He didn't tell her about his suspicions that Dr. Lieber was using the local men who were already very sick as white mice for his chelation experiments. He certainly didn't tell her that Dr. Lieber was apparently considering her as a subject for his increasingly aggressive treatment.

"I'm going to run up to see Marcus Steamer this evening. He wants me to educate him a little about Dr. Lieber's notes, I guess." Tomas said. "Do you think you can handle this little baby by yourself?

Spirit was practically in tears with frustration. Her breasts were hard and painful with the initial congestion of milk. Her abdomen hurt where the incision had been made, and having an infant, even one as tiny as her daughter, digging her little heels and toes into the bandages protecting the wound, was not helping. She felt swollen and exhausted. She looked up at Tomas with what she hoped was calm determination. "Of course I'll be fine. How much trouble can a five pound baby make? But I thought that the Lieber matter was solved. What happened?"

"From what I hear, what the police thought to be the murder weapon turned out not to be the murder weapon. The bullets didn't match up with Bonnie's gun."

Spirit was impressed. She was itching to get involved, and to defend Bonnie if possible. She couldn't believe that Bonnie, who she knew as well as she knew anyone in the county, had it in her to hurt anyone.

"How is Bonnie?" she asked.

Tomas shook his head. "Not good. Not good at all. She's still in the hospital, and from what Clara says she is just sinking further into herself. She is hardly talking to anyone. Most of the time she just sits there all day. She says she doesn't remember anything about the time after her dad died."

"The poor thing."

"Yes, and it's destroying Clara. She is trying to take care of Clay, and without any help now that her sisters have gone back to their homes."

Spirit's eyes overflowed. Tomas saw the tears and decided

to change the subject. "Speaking of homes," he said. "Ed says it is time to put some furniture in that house."

Spirit wiped her face with a hospital washcloth and smiled weakly at Tomas. "When do you think I can go home?" she asked.

"I'll talk to the doctor," he said. "Maybe they'll let you out tomorrow, especially if I promise to take good care of you two."

Tomas kissed the top of Spirit's head. The smell of her hair was like home to him, and he knew that as excited as he was to move into the new home it was mainly for her and the baby. "Luz," he said out loud.

Spirit looked up "What?" she said.

"Luz," Tomas said. "I want to name her "Luz.""

"That's a Spanish name."

"I know that. It means light."

"I know."

"So what do you think?"

Spirit said nothing for a moment. She held the child up and away from her. The eyes that had been squeezed shut for most of the past days opened and it was as if the round face lit up with life. Spirit took it as a sign. "Luz Soledad Hotone," she said to the baby. "What do you think?"

As if on cue the baby opened her starfish fingers and seemed to reach out to her enthralled parents. They looked at each other and laughed.

"I think she likes it," Spirit said.

* * *

At the Chicken Coop, Possum was the talk of the early morning regular coffee drinking crowd. Some began to place bets on what color his hair would be the next week. Possum enjoyed the attention and played along. So far he had been splotchy-blonde, then bright red all over, and after that, shoe-polish black. Gigi became the boss of his hair; Possum went along with whatever she wanted that would keep him under her fingertips. The help he had provided to Deputy--no, Sheriff Weatherford had boosted Possum's reputation, and it wouldn't be long before Possum might legitimately claim to be *going out with Gigi*.

When the regulars weren't placing friendly bets on the next color of Possum's stubble, they were talking about the murder of Dr. Lieber, or the death of the Sheriff. Nick Costa listened when he could from the privacy of the grill area, but never offered any opinion on what was going to happen to poor Bonnie. Possum reminded anyone who hadn't already heard the story a half dozen times about how he had found the gun--even though by now he knew that he shouldn't have moved it; Dan lectured him heavily about that. Privately, Nick believed if Bonnie could get a good lawyer, like Sprite, she would never spend a day in jail for the murder. After it became known that Bonnie's gun was not the one that shot Dr. Lieber, he would have bet money that she would never be convicted.

* * *

Marcus Steamer needed all the help he could get in putting together the information and the evidence on Dr. Lieber's murder. He gave Tomas a copy of the medical records and notes. He called in Dan Weatherford to discuss the physical evidence. They discussed the jurisdictional issues: should the prosecution be in the County where the murder was committed, or the County in which the accused lived, or in a tribal tribunal? And what about the mismatch between the gun and the bullets? What was to be made of that inconvenient truth?

Tomas wasn't bogged down by the jurisdictional issues. He read the computer records long into the night and by morning had come to an ugly conclusion: Dr. Lieber was running dangerous experiments on a group of highly vulnerable men and women in a remote location. And he was using the local mining companies as a scapegoat. He made sure that each of the subjects who received his accelerated therapy had been employed by a company that had exposed them to carcinogenic agents in the past. Then he made a lot of noise in the media and the medical journals pointing an accusatory finger at companies like the Kingman Brick Company or even the U.S. government in its weapons testing at Sandia--all to distract attention from his egotistical rush to claim a cure for certain cancers. The unbridled ego of the man. How could anyone be so hungry for fame?

And to think he was ready to expand his project to practice on Spirit, and on Luz.

Tomas wrote a lengthy e-mail to Marcus Steamer, outlining his conclusions, and referencing the appropriate files, notes, e-mails and copies of speeches and public testimony. At dawn he sent the file to Marcus and settled in to a deep sleep.

* * *

Tomas took Spirit and Luz home, first to the trailer and soon after, to the new home in the hills. Tomas and Sprite had only two good hands between them, and Sprite was still limited in what she could to. "No heavy lifting for six weeks," her surgeon told her. And so they took their time in packing their belongings and hauling Spirit's furniture and bicycle and books and pots and pans to the new house. Dan Weatherford pitched in and proved to be invaluable as they tried to set up the bed frame and put together a crib for Luz.

Spirit invited Dan to stay for supper after the long moving day, and he gratefully accepted. He needed to talk to Spirit about his conversation with the Sheriff as he lay dying, and to make a plan for what to do next with Kingman Brick Company, when Cal Kingman came looking for help.

They would wait until that happened, they decided, and then they would take their information to the State's Attorney. Spirit poured a small glass of wine for herself, Dan Weatherford and Tomas. They toasted to new beginnings, for Dan's future as the Sheriff, for the new home, and most important, for Luz Soledad Hotone.

Dan left for his own home with a vague feeling of envy for Sprite and Tomas. They were in love, the baby was perfect and the new house was gorgeous. Suddenly his own small, used house and his sour, resentful wife had all the appeal of a broken down used car. Dan tried to push the thoughts from his mind; he was sincerely happy for his friends, he just wished that he had that kind of bliss for himself. It had been a very long time since he longed to be in his wife's arms, whispering into each other's ears before falling into a deep and happy sleep. He felt old. His disappointment over Hank's near confession lingered as a depressing ending to a treasured friendship. With a deep sigh, he pulled into his driveway and steeled himself for another evening with his wife.

* * *

Bonnie was finally able to go to bed. The floor nurses kept everyone in the day room until 9:00 p.m., when they were able to go to their rooms and read or talk with their roommates, take a shower if they wished, write letters or make entries in their therapy journals. At ten o'clock it was lights out. From her narrow hospital bed Bonnie could see the full moon. It was what used to be her favorite time of the month. A full moon always lifted her creativity and her sensitivity. Now she had no favorite time of the month. Also no favorite movie, or song, or food. The world seemed two dimensional, flat and uninteresting.

She should be missing her little boy, but she really didn't. The medication that she was taking since she arrived at the hospital took away her feelings about almost everything. She couldn't cry but she couldn't laugh either. The other patients said the medication was weird shit. She could not disagree, but neither did she have any feeling about having to take the medicine.

Eat, sleep, take a shower, see the doctor, take the medicine, eat, sleep, take a shower. The days dragged on, and as another one passed just the same as the day before, with Bonnie no closer to happy or alive than the day before that, she wondered if she would ever want to live again.

Her life before the hospital or maybe before the healing ceremony or maybe before her dad got sick, seemed to have happened to someone else. If she were to get out of the hospital, where would she go? Where could she go, and be allowed to eat, sleep, take medicine, and then begin all over again.

Bonnie pulled the sheet and blanket completely over her

head. She didn't want to see the moon. It reminded her of when she was alive.

Chapter 31

Dan Weatherford eyed the small sturdy box containing the remains of Sheriff Andrews and decided it was time for them to go home. He loaded the box into the trunk of the squad car and drove slower than usual to Hank's house. He was surprised to see a Ford Tempo in the drive with Ohio plates.

The garage door was open and inside he could see a man who looked like Hank-- with more hair. The man looked up when Dan's cruiser turned in the drive. He wiped his hands on a rag and came out into the crisp sunlight.

Dan extended his hand and said, "I'm Dan Weatherford."

The man studied Dan's open face and decided he was there as a friend. "Bobby Andrews," he said. "Hank was my brother."

"I'm very sorry about Hank. He was my boss but he was also my friend."

Bobby passed his hand over his head to pat down a section of hair that threatened to break loose in the brisk wind. "This is sure some wind you have out here," he said.

Dan glanced at the plates on the car. "You came in from Ohio, then."

"Yes. Hank's ex-wife called me and told me about Hank. I didn't even know that he was sick."

"I guess he didn't know either. Of course it was the infection that got him, more than anything."

Bobby nodded. "That's what I heard."

"I'm glad that someone from the family is here. I was just bringing Hank's ashes over to the house. It didn't seem right to keep them at the office."

Dan walked to the trunk of his car and raised the lid. He

pulled out Hank's box and gave it to Bobby. "He wanted his gun to be buried with him so it is all in there."

Bobby took the box into the garage and set it on Hank's workbench.

"I've got something too," he said. "I don't know what to do with this but it looked important." He pulled a metal lockbox from a tool cabinet and set in on the workbench next to Hank's ashes. The box had a combination lock. "I've tried a few combinations to try to open it but nothing worked."

"We could try to break the lock here, but I think that there is a guy back at the department who could get into it a lot easier."

"Why don't you just take it? Of course if it is full of money I want it back," he said with a laugh.

Dan agreed. "There will be a memorial service at the department. I'm not sure of the date yet. Are you going to be staying around here for a while?"

"I will be. I'm about the only blood family that Hank had. And I'm retired so I have the time to figure out what to do with his furniture and stuff."

Dan was relieved that he would not have to be the one to do that. "Well that's great." He took out his wallet and thumbed through the bills compartment and drew out a business card, and then he took out a pen from his breast pocket and wrote his home phone number on it. "Let me know if I can help," he said.

"I'll be in touch about the box after we get it open," he said.

Bobby's mind was already on the job to be done but he shook hands again with Dan, and said, "Thanks again."

Back at the office, Dan placed the firebox in the center of Hank's desk. He called the bomb squad specialist and asked him to come by and explained the situation. "No problem," said the specialist. I'll do it this morning, got nothing else to do."

Dan was running late for a meeting with Marcus Steamer and the Waipiti County State's Attorney. A decision was to be made about prosecuting Bonnie.

When he arrived the others were drinking coffee and analyzing the game from the night before. The Cowboys had stomped the Broncos, 36-7. It was the Cowboys strong defense that had carried the game, though. The Broncos were close to scoring on several occasions, and were pushed back by the Cowboys massive linemen. Nobody thought that the Cowboys had an offense capable of beating some of the other teams that they faced between then and the Superbowl.

They got down to business eventually. Dan and Marcus laid out the case and they argued first about where the trial should be brought.

Marcus Steamer didn't press too hard for tribal jurisdiction. After what Tomas had told him about Dr. Lieber's experiments on some of his people, and on Bonnie's father himself, he couldn't much blame her for plugging him. He also knew that where Bonnie was now was punishment enough. He really didn't feel like arresting a broken woman. She was not likely to be a danger to anyone other than herself.

The Waipiti County State's Attorney needed a big trial in the next year. He was eyeballing the chance to run for Lieutenant Governor the following year and he would prosecute the hell out of anyone who had murdered a heroic doctor in such a cold way, murder weapon or no murder weapon. If Dr. Lieber's blood was found on Bonnie's jeans, for God's sake, she could hide out in the psych ward all she wanted, he was going after her. She would be assigned a public defender, but the state's attorney couldn't think of any one of them that could match his prosecutorial skills. Bring it on, he thought.

Dan Weatherford received a call on his cell phone from his office. The bomb squad specialist had opened the box. Dan picked up his hat and excused himself. It looked like the State's Attorney had made his decision, anyway. With a nod to Marcus Steamer, he ducked out of the conference room.

The lockbox was back on the Sheriff's desk. Dan opened the lid and saw a stack of black leather ledgers. He drew out the top one and opened it to the first light green page. At the top was an entry: January 1, 2001 - January 31, 2001. In Hank's handwriting, the page contained five columns. The headings were underlined and neatly spaced and outlined specific payments made to the Sheriff. The dates, amounts, purposes and source showed a pattern of off book payments going back many years.

He closed the book on 2001 and flipped through the stack, noting the perfect order they were in. The ledgers spanned almost thirty years of Sheriff Andrews' political career.

He drew out another ledger at random and opened it, wetting his finger and turning the pages. He saw the name Kingman Brick Company on June 16, 1974 and continuing on he noticed it again in September 3, 1974.

His hands shaking, Dan closed the ledger and sat down in the Sheriff's padded leather chair. He shouldn't jump to conclusions. The careful records might show a lifetime pattern of wrongdoing, or only private records of campaign contributions. Dan felt the sudden urge to talk these things over with Sprite. He picked up the phone and dialed her number.

* * *

Make the world go away, thought Sprite, when she heard the telephone ring.

She was sitting in the birch wood rocker that had been a surprise gift from Ed, their builder who became their friend during the hectic weeks of completing the home, their home. There was little other furniture in the high ceilinged family room, and that was fine with her. She had pulled the rocker close to the window and was holding Luz. The baby was snuggled deep into a crocheted white blanket that matched her cap and booties. Spirit had been making up a song for her when the phone rang.

But the telephone didn't go away. Sprite pushed herself with her one good hand out of the chair as she balanced the baby between her body and the cast on her left arm.

When she saw that the caller was Dan Weatherford, she didn't resent the intrusion. She always enjoyed talking with Dan.

"Sheriff Weatherford," Sprite said.

"Hi, Sprite," he said. "How are the girls today?"

"We're doing well today," said Spirit. It was almost true.

Tomas had finally told her about the extent of the surgery and tearfully explained that she would have no more children. Spirit was still recovering from that shock, but she knew that she should be celebrating the most important discovery: the tumor was benign. It was massive, and dangerous, but she didn't have cancer. And her Luz was shining brightly.

Dan was on his way to visit. He said he was bringing some information that he had just received that he needed Sprite to look over. "It's going to keep you busy for a while."

Sprite protested, and joked, "I've only got two, no – only one hand! Dan soothed her, saying, "Don't worry, there is no rush."

* * *

And then he was there at her dining room table. Tomas would be home by dinnertime, he had gone to Hidden City to order some cabinets and shelves for the garage. Dan didn't want to take any more of Sprite's time than he had to, so he was going to get right to the point. And then he remembered the morning meeting about Bonnie.

"This isn't why I came, but you would want to know that Bonnie is going to be prosecuted. The State's Attorney seems to be interested in winning a big case this year."

Sprite sat quietly for a moment, and then said, "Isn't there any way that you can talk him out of it, Dan?"

Dan took her right hand in his. "Sprite, my first duty is to uphold the law."

She interrupted, "You saw her. She was out of her right mind. She is sick, Dan, and you know it."

Quietly Dan said, "Even if she is sick, I believe that she killed Terry Lieber. She as much as confessed that to me."

She looked into Dan's face. "If she is prosecuted, I'm going to defend her, if she wants me to."

Dan held her gaze. "Counselor, I was hoping you would say that."

There was a long silence. Luz was the first one to "speak" when she woke up and began to make a series of baby sounds that broke abruptly into a rising wail.

It broke the tension. "Dan, excuse me for a moment. I'm starting to understand Luz' cries. That's the hungry-baby yell."

Dan smiled. He remembered his own babies, and how his wife claimed she could tell the difference between I'm hurt and feed me. To Dan, it was all noise. "Thank goodness for mothers," he said.

To give the new mom her privacy, Dan walked to the plate glass window that revealed the breathtaking view of the ravine. He was tracing the bent trunk of one tree when he noticed the chalky outline of a petroglyph. Dan grew excited. He turned to Sprite.

"Have you noticed that drawing on the other side of the ravine?"

"Oh yes, said Sprite, "I was trying to get a better look at it the day I was dancing and tripped. She raised her casted arm. With this I have had to put that plan on hold.

Dan looked at it again. "Do you happen to have any binoculars?" he asked.

"You know, we do," said Sprite. "I think that Tomas put them in the desk drawer in his office."

"May I get them? I'd like to have a closer look. I've always been fascinated by the drawings."

"Of course, just go look in the right hand desk drawer."

While Sprite nursed Luz, Dan studied the figure. "It's an owl," He said finally.

Sprite was surprised and pleased. "I was afraid it was a hawk," she said. A hawk figure would have been a warning sign, a bad omen. But an owl--they would be protected, even in the night. Her spirits lifted. An owl would bring wisdom, as well as protection.

Sprite noticed the box on the floor near the door, "What is it you brought, Dan?"

Dan had been so distracted by the talk about Bonnie, and then by the baby's crying, and the petroglyph, that his original mission was almost forgotten.

"Oh, yes. Sprite, Hank's brother found a lock box while he was packing up Hank's things. He asked me to open it --it was locked and had to be opened by one of our staff --and there are records --very detailed, very thorough records going back to the beginning of Hank's campaigns. They show every penny that Hank ever received, who it was from, and what's was for.

Sprite arched both eyebrows and looked meaningfully at Dan. "

"Did you happen to see anything from Kingman Brick Company?"

"I did. I didn't look through every journal, but one that I randomly picked out-I think it was from 1974, had at least two entries from Kingman."

Sprite closed her eyes and rocked. "We can easily match those with the thank you cards, and make some sense of the case."

"And you thought you could retire into motherhood. We need you to get back to work, Sprite. I need you."

"Can you leave the box with me for a while? I'm going to need to take care of this little later along with taking on the politics of Waipiti County, if it comes to that."

"Take all the time you need. I've got plenty of work to catch up on."

"I'm sure you do, Sheriff."

"Let me know if you need help."

Sprite held up her cast. "At least I'll be getting this lump of plaster off my arm real soon."

Dan put his broad brimmed hat on and tipped the edge in a hint of salute to Sprite. She returned the salute, then gave him an awkward hug.

She closed the door behind Dan. The house was quiet. She would have to get used to the echoes of the large rooms.

Sprite picked up Luz and took her to the window. She pointed the baby toward the view of the owl figure. "We'll need all the protection and wisdom that we can get, won't we, Luz." She smiled at her daughter, and for the first time, her daughter smiled back. It was like the sun breaking from behind the snow filled clouds.

* * *

On his way back to Desert View, Tomas stopped by Clara's house. He had taken to checking on her. She was always glad to see Tomas, and deeply appreciated his willingness to help her with some home chore that Bonnie or Jim had always done. Last time it was putting on a couple of storm windows. Today he had brought some groceries.

Clara was not the only one who was happy to see Tomas. Her grandson Clay had attached himself like a puppy to the older man, and came running from wherever he had been playing as soon as he heard the sound of Tomas' car. Tomas always dropped down on one knee, scooping Clay up and sailing him through the air. "Hello sonny," Tomas said with a broad smile.

Clara would look at him with her lips pressed together, silently watching them. She remembered her vision of Tomas with a small boy and wondered at the mysteries of life.

Sources:

1. Collier, John.
Patterns and Ceremonials of the Indians of the Southwest.
New York: Dover Publications, Inc. 1995 edition.

2. Jahoda, Gloria.
The Trail of Tears.
New York: New York: Random House, 1995 edition.

3. Mooney, James.
Myths of the Cherokee,
New York: Dover Publications, Inc. 1995 edition.

4. Shimer, Porter.
Healing Secrets of the Native Americans.
Owing Mills, Maryland:
Tess Press, 1999 edition.

5. Author/s unknown for the poems quoted in part in this book and attributed elsewhere to the Navajo Nation, from various chanting ceremonies described as the Beautyway, Blessingway, and Nightway.

www.ingramcontent.com/pod-product-compliance
Lightning Source LLC
Chambersburg PA
CBHW061200170626
46809CB00003B/1186